ES

"HEY! WHAT ARE YOU DOING?"

Jessica's startled question was cut off as he pulled her onto his lap in one deft motion. He grasped the back of her neck and she found her face against his tanned throat.

She managed to get free enough to protest, "For Pete's sake—let go of me. I can't breathe!"

"Calm down," came his firm voice in her ear. "You're breathing." His clasp tightened and he lowered his lips to hers. Jessica's last resistance disappeared under mounting delight.

"I can hardly believe this is really happening—I've dreamed it for so long," she whispered.

"Stop dreaming . . . this is for real. . . ."

The
Marrying Kind

Glenna Finley

A SIGNET BOOK

NEW AMERICAN LIBRARY

A DIVISION OF PENGUIN BOOKS USA INC.

PUBLISHER'S NOTE

NAL BOOKS ARE AVAILABLE AT QUANTITY DISCOUNTS WHEN USED TO PROMOTE PRODUCTS OR SERVICES. FOR INFORMATION PLEASE WRITE TO PREMIUM MARKETING DIVISION, NEW AMERICAN LIBRARY, 1633 BROADWAY, NEW YORK, NEW YORK 10019.

SIGNET TRADEMARK REG. U.S. PAT. OFF. AND FOREIGN COUNTRIES
REGISTERED TRADEMARK—MARCA REGISTRADA
HECHO EN DRESDEN, TN

SIGNET, SIGNET CLASSIC, MENTOR, ONYX, PLUME, MERIDIAN and NAL BOOKS are published by New American Library, a division of Penguin Books USA Inc., 1633 Broadway, New York, New York 10019

First Printing, July, 1989

1 2 3 4 5 6 7 8 9

PRINTED IN THE UNITED STATES OF AMERICA

Marriage and hanging go by destiny;
matches are made in heaven.
                                    —Burton

1

Jessica Webster stared at the throngs of people around her and shook her head in disbelief, wondering when the expression "getting away from it all" became synonymous with a trip beyond the city limits.

Not that she'd expected a lonely journey when she'd driven north on the freeway from Seattle that August morning to connect with the big Washington State ferry that serviced the San Juan Islands. Isolation wasn't on the list of attractions for the scattering of islets any longer—not since the travel editors had featured the northwest corner of the United States as a wonderful undiscovered vacation area and their faithful readers had flocked there in droves.

It was just as well that some of those editors weren't around to see what their handiwork had accomplished, Jessica thought as she looked around the mainland ferry terminal trying to find an unoccupied spot. When an overweight man stood up, tossed his duffel bag over his shoulder, and headed for the coffee bar, Jessica slid thankfully into his former seat on the bench. Her satisfied expression lasted only a moment, however, before an announcement came over the public-address system that the ferry for

Friday Harbor would be delayed another twenty minutes.

She thought bitterly of the early-morning wake-up call at her Seattle motel and the hurried toast-and-coffee breakfast gulped at a freeway stop—all to be early for a ferry that was running late. "Dammit! I should have known!" she muttered, bestowing a bitter glance on the public-address speaker.

An older woman sitting next to her in the midst of a collection of luggage regarded Jessica ruefully. "I can tell you've taken this ferry before," she said.

Jessica turned to give her a halfhearted smile. "Not for a while, but it's been a long morning and we haven't even started yet."

"That's not unusual at this time of the year," the woman said. "I never thought the San Juans would have a 'high season,' but it's getting more crowded all the time on the islands. Are you staying long?"

"Not very," Jessica said, keeping her tone pleasant since her seatmate was clearly trying to make the waiting pass a little faster. "I'm looking up old friends while I take a short vacation break."

"At least you picked a good time for it. The weather's been lovely all month." The older woman leaned back, thinking that the visitor's short vacation wouldn't be spent alone. Not with such thick wavy dark red hair curling over her collar, and that porcelain complexion. No wonder more than one man in the terminal was looking her way. There was an understated elegance about her, too, one that wasn't often found in a woman in her mid-twenties. That cool, clear, polite voice added to it, and her clothes completed the picture. The gray gabardine slacks and matching tailored silk shirt were not only chic but fitted her to perfection. A pale yellow jacket draped carelessly around her shoulders finished the illusion. At the moment, there wasn't much hope of continuing the conversation because the subject of her attention had closed her eyes to rest her head against the wooden bench, showing a profile of a small straight nose and delicately firm chin.

Jessica had no idea that she was a source of interest to anyone as she tried to get comfortable on the hard bench. It was really the first time she'd relaxed since she'd left Dallas the day before and flown to Seattle. By the time she'd completed the formalities for her rental car and checked into an airport motel at Sea-Tac, there was only time for a hamburger in the coffee shop before going to bed.

No one in the ferry terminal would have suspected that Jessica's inner feelings were nowhere near as assured as her outer appearance indicated. Until that moment, her tight travel schedule had pushed her concerns to the back of her mind, but the delay gave them a chance to come flooding back.

It had been years since she'd last visited San Juan Island, and then it was a far happier occasion—a family reunion at her grandmother's home. To her eight-year-old mind, the island had been the most delightful of playgrounds and she had cried when the holiday was over. Years later, after her grandmother died, her parents had decided to move to the family property but they had both died tragically in an automobile accident en route to the Northwest. Jessica's brother Tom had handled all the arrangements after that, agreeing to lease the big island home, since neither he nor Jessica wanted to face the painful memories that were synonymous with it.

After Tom had moved to Hong Kong in connection with his export-import firm the year before, he'd told Jessica to do what she wanted with the house. "I doubt if I'll get up there for a decent vacation—much as I'd like to," he'd confessed on one of his rare trips back to Texas for a business conference. "I know there's no point in renting it forever while the property just deteriorates. But it's up to you," he'd said quickly on seeing her disheartened expression. "I'll go along with whatever you decide. S'matter of fact, I'll even sign my half of the house over to you if that'll make things easier." He'd given her a slow grin. "Better take me up on the idea while I'm still in a weak state of mind."

"No chance," she'd replied firmly. "The only way I'd do that would be to buy your half, and I can't afford it. Let's wait and see—then make up our minds."

"You're sure that you want to spend your vacation up there?"

"I want to, but I don't think Henry's keen on the idea. He's still giving me an argument."

"I'm surprised that he joined the world long enough to even answer your letter."

"Probably his secretary reminded him," Jessica had replied with resignation. "He hasn't changed a bit over the years so far as I can see, and he's lived in the house for so long that he probably thinks he owns it."

"I *told* you that we should have charged him more rent. Then he'd remember."

"Well, he's your old college chum—not mine. Besides, if you get beyond that absentminded exterior, he's all right. From what I've read in the papers, he's the shining light of all the ecological devotees on the island these days. The research he's done on that Orca whale pod even made national television."

"Did you see it?"

"No—but he sent me some of the publicity after I wrote and said that I wanted to occupy the house for a week or so. There was a P.S. at the bottom of his letter to say he could stay aboard the Institute's research boat if my trip was really necessary, but he hoped it wouldn't be an extended visit."

Tom burst out laughing. "He hasn't changed. Don't let him con you into picking up the check if you find yourself in the same restaurant."

"I'll remember."

Going over that conversation in her mind didn't do anything to ease Jessica's thoughts just then. Her public-relations job in Dallas was high-powered and hard on the digestion. The hurried flight to the Northwest and the long drive on the freeway hadn't helped, and she had to make a conscious effort to relax as she opened her eyes to stare out the big windows of the ferry terminal onto the water.

At least she'd been lucky in terms of the weather. It was one of those rare picture-perfect days that made the natives beam with pride while hoping that not many visitors would consider moving there permanently. Sunlight dappled the calm cove which was the mainland ferry terminus, and beyond, she could see a few of the one hundred and seventy-two islands of the vacation land. Gently rolling green terrain and the boat-dotted blue waters could have been framed for a travel poster. Through a fluke of geography, the ribbon of islands boasted a drier and more gentle climate than the mainland. As a result, the myriad coves and harbors made the area a sailor's paradise and a weekender's delight. No one was really surprised when the famed Orca pod of whales had decided to make their home there too.

Jessica just wished that she had a month or two to

enjoy the halcyon surroundings without disturbing Henry Carter. He'd been a friend of her brother's so long that she ignored his idiosyncrasies—knowing that underneath his egghead exterior he was a kindly soul. Although, knowing Henry, she wouldn't be surprised to learn that he'd already planned to take over his secretary's lodging place and force the poor woman to bunk with relatives.

A sudden stir of the people in the terminal heralded the appearance of a big green-and-white Washington State ferry in the cove. The voice over the public-address system advised foot passengers for San Juan Island that they could proceed to the overhead ramp and be ready to board shortly.

Jessica picked up her small suitcase and managed to get the big tote bag over her shoulder without staggering before following the serpentine of people going up the ramp. A quick glimpse over the railing made her thankful that she hadn't attempted to bring her car on board, since the lineup of automobiles extended almost to the top of the hill two blocks away.

Which is getting away from it all with a vengeance, she told herself cynically. Just like the middle of Times Square or a campground where people shared common tent stakes.

She waited in line for the debarking ferry passengers to file past and started to giggle as she surveyed some of their outfits. Evidently "flower children" hadn't disappeared from the scene as completely as she'd imagined. Either that or some craft shop on the island had an "end-of-the-season" sale of batik and thong sandals, because a goodly percentage of long-haired women were wearing them. When combined with tight T-shirts worn au naturel it was enough to make Thoreau retreat deeper in Walden and Rip Van Winkle try for another hundred.

Some of the men weren't much better; their choices of baby-pink shorts or red-and-white striped ensembles made Jessica shake her head. She only hoped that they had some jeans stuffed in their duffel bags in case the weather changed as quickly as it often did.

At that moment the line of people started to move slowly up the ramp, and a little later she handed her ticket to the official on the upper level of the super-ferry.

The fresh-air lovers immediately found seats on the open deck, while the rest of the passengers surged through the doors into the covered section amidships. There was a split again when a large group of passengers veered off into the coffee shop, where the smell of hamburgers announced that breakfast was being replaced by lunch.

Jessica moved on, observing that the bench sections next to the huge ferry windows were already occupied, but she was content to settle into a chair in the center section and stow her baggage around her feet.

As she reached for a book in the side pocket of her tote bag, a toddler was plunked into the seat beside her by his mother with the admonition to "Sit there and behave." The woman, who appeared to be in her late teens, immediately took off toward the coffee shop, leaving the little boy with only a wooden toy to amuse himself.

It didn't hold his attention for long and, after seeing him lurch down the row of chairs toward some other youngsters who were playing in the aisle, Jessica let out her breath in relief and concentrated on her book.

She was brought out of it rudely sometime later when the youngster was deposited in front of her by a tall dark-haired man wearing jeans and a blue crewneck sweater. "You'd better do more baby-sitting and less reading," he admonished her, watching the subdued youngster crawl quickly into the empty chair. "He was doing his damnedest to reach the top of the railing over the stern a minute ago."

Jessica drew in a startled breath. "I had no idea—"

He cut into her words rudely. "I don't imagine you did. At least he knew where he belonged." His glance turned to the youngster, who was once again engrossed in the toy he was balancing on the chair arm. "It's a good thing he doesn't know how close he came."

Then, before Jessica had a chance to proclaim her innocence, the boy's rescuer turned abruptly and strode away amidship. As Jessica watched, he greeted one of the ferry's officers and they both disappeared through a door marked "Crew Only."

"Of all the self-righteous prigs!" Jessica's temper stirred belatedly at the injustice of it all even as she saw the boy's mother strolling toward them, a bag of potato chips in one hand and a soft drink in the other.

The toddler launched himself toward her and Jessica quickly decided there must be more pleasant places for the remainder of the voyage. She stowed her things against a convenient bulkhead and marched down to the coffee shop—deciding a change of scene would help her ignore the undeserved dressing-down. As she selected a doughnut and poured a cup of coffee, she was mentally rehearsing just what she should have said to that unpleasant male who'd judged her guilty without a trial.

She managed to find a small table at the back of the dining enclosure where she could watch the passersby and still see out the big square ferry window onto the islands, which were just a stone's throw beyond the railing.

The scenery was so spectacular that she forgot her annoyance for the moment, completely enthralled by the combination of land and water topped with the pale blue summer sky. Most of the islands had secluded coves where pleasure boats were moored in front of vacation property. The homes were barely visible through the camouflage of trees which most property owners had left undisturbed for privacy. Jessica frowned as she tried to remember the names of the islands; that must have been Lopez off to the left, which meant that Orcas would be coming up to the starboard. For an instant she considered leaving her coffee to go and check the other side of the ferry, and then decided against it. It was peaceful where she was, and there probably would be plenty of time during the week for a jaunt to the other islands.

She took another sip of coffee and tried to ignore the fact that she didn't really want to run the risk of encountering her critic again. God knows, he'd probably fix her with another accusing glare or pair her up with another misbehaving child. Not that she made a habit of ignominious retreats, but just then the prospect of peace and quiet was more attractive than picking up any gauntlets. She finished her doughnut, dusted her fingers on a paper napkin, and opened her book, deciding that the heroine could have all the adventures until they reached San Juan Island.

It was another half-hour before the sudden surge of passengers toward the car decks of the vessel made

Jessica decide it was time to retrieve her belongings and get ready for debarkation.

This time, she had to go down to the lower deck, and there was time once she reached it to wander over by the railing and survey the harbor the ferry was entering. Her eyes widened as she saw the number of pleasure craft anchored in the various marinas. The sight of a sprawling new building at the water's edge about a mile from the main part of town prompted her to strike up a conversation with a middle-aged couple standing beside her.

"Excuse me," she said with a smile, "but I wonder if you could tell me what that building is? It's new since the last time I was here."

"It's the North Pacific Marine Institute—a private research organization," the man replied promptly. "It was just built a couple of years ago. There was quite a fuss at the time. Most of the folks who live here didn't want to have anything that big coming in on a permanent basis."

Jessica's smile widened. "You sound like one of those folks."

"I didn't realize it showed so much," the man's wife said with a reproving glance at her husband. "Actually, the people who work there have helped the economy and, for the most part, they seem to keep to themselves."

"They may, but their work is in the headlines most of the time," her husband reminded her. "That means there are usually reporters hanging around."

"He's right about that," the woman told Jessica. "I suppose it helps the Institute people to get the government grants they need for research, but most of us who live here could do with a little less publicity about the island. A couple of years ago, you wouldn't have found half this many people on the ferry." She gestured to encompass the crowds waiting by the chain so they'd be first off when the vessel finally docked. "And speaking of people, we'd better gather the kids and get in the van," she admonished her husband. "I wonder where Sue-Lynn and Todd went? I told them to stay close. Neighbor kids," she added for Jessica's benefit. "They wanted to go to the mainland for the ride."

"They're back there talking to those other youngsters," the man said, pointing toward the stairs. "Make it fast, though. I need your help rearranging the stuff in the car," he said over his shoulder as he started toward a van parked nearby.

"I'll go get them," Jessica offered. "Just tell me which ones they are."

"Would you?" The woman beamed. "It would help a lot. Tell them Retha and Jim want them in the car now. They're the little Oriental girl in the plaid shirt and the boy next to her wearing the rust-colored denims." She indicated the two small children, who were giggling at the antics of a Great Dane whose head protruded through the sun roof of an expensive sports car.

"I'll be glad to." Jessica noted where the couple's van was located and then made her way back through the tightly parked cars to the children. "C'mon, kids, you're supposed to be in the van. Retha and Jim want you right away."

"Okay." Sue-Lynn turned obediently toward the bow of the ferry, and then paused to say importantly, "You'll have to carry Todd, he's a slowpoke."

"Is that right, young man?" Jessica asked the black toddler, who grinned back at her. He looked to be about four years old and didn't appear in the least put out by Sue-Lynn's accusation. Instead, he simply held up his arms.

"Good idea," Jessica said, giving silent thanks that her tote bag had a broad shoulder strap so that it could be shoved out of the way. "You must have had two breakfasts, you're a lump," she told Todd once she'd hoisted him up. "Lead on, Sue-Lynn."

"Lump, lump, lump," Todd chattered happily in her ear as they followed the other passengers who'd started forward as chains rattled near the bow, signifying that the docking was complete. Jessica noted absently that Sue-Lynn was almost treading on the heels of the boy who'd been racing around the upper deck earlier. At least his mother was close by this time, she thought thankfully as they followed in a narrow line through the cars that were being started on either side of them.

Jessica glanced casually into a gray car and then did an almost comic double-take as she recognized the man in the driver's seat. Later she was to thank her stars that he didn't notice her startled surprise, since he was staring unbelievingly at the three children around her—the little towheaded boy from the upper deck, who was bound for a station wagon, the bright-eyed Korean girl, and then the black toddler in her arms.

Their glance met just a moment and then his mouth settled in a firm line as he realized that he'd given himself away. Jessica moved quickly on, hoping that she'd be out of sight before laughter overcame her.

Fortunately the van was on the other side of a ventilating column. When Sue-Lynn and Todd were stowed safely into it, there was only time for a hasty good-bye before the line of cars moved on.

She took her time going back around the bulkhead

to retrieve her suitcase, and was happy to see that the car with her accuser in it was halfway up the wooden pier.

"So much for you, my friend," she said in an undertone, and started up the side of the dock herself, in the most cheerful frame of mind since she'd begun the trip. Instead of being able to set Mr. Know-it-all straight, she'd given him something else to think about. It was a pity she couldn't have heard his reaction to this one, because from the look on his face, it would have been a lulu!

She fell in line with the last stragglers—not in any hurry to reach the street, where foot passengers from the ferry were being met and a stubby little bus that serviced the other parts of the island was rapidly filling up.

Jessica stared around her, trying to remember if the landing area had changed at all in the intervening years, and then shook her head impatiently. Of course it had, and it wasn't surprising.

There was no use wallowing in nostalgia; she'd be better just to go about the business of selling the family property and then get on with the rest of her life.

Having made her decision, it was frustrating to stand on the curb and look in vain for the transportation she'd thought would be waiting. She looked around again, trying to determine if any of the tall fair-haired men in view could possibly be Henry Carter. Of course, it didn't have to be Henry—she'd merely sent him a note at the last minute stating her ferry's arrival time and asking that he arrange for transportation to get her to the house.

After another ten minutes went by, her lips thinned in annoyance and she picked up her bag, searching the surroundings for a phone to call a taxi.

There were two seafood restaurants nearby overlooking the harbor, but they didn't look as if they'd have phones in the foyer. Her steps slowed as she stared across at the long municipal pier where literally hundreds of pleasure craft were tied up. There'd be phones there somewhere on the dock, but it was a long hot walk to carry a suitcase.

She'd give him five more minutes and then she'd definitely make a move. She should have remembered that the only thing Henry had ever managed in the past was to drop in for dinner at precisely the right time.

Exactly four minutes had gone by and she was just reaching down to pick up her bag when a disreputable pickup truck stopped at the curb by her. Jessica looked up idly as the driver leaned across to the open window and said in a well-remembered icy tone, "You wouldn't happen to know if there's a Jessica Webster around?"

Jessica was so stunned at seeing her dark-haired critic from the ferry that she heard herself saying idiotically, "You've changed cars. You weren't driving that truck off the ferry."

"You've changed too," he said laconically. "Where did you stash your kids this time?"

For a moment she toyed with carrying on the charade and then abandoned the idea. Standing in the hot sun waiting for her ride had caused the last vestige of humor to dry up. She eyed her accuser with a disdain that should have shriveled him as she replied, "I presume they're with their parents. At least they were the last time I saw them."

"You mean they weren't—"

"Mine?" She shook her head and finished the sentence before he had a chance. "Wrong all the way around. So the next time you start lecturing a woman, make sure of your facts."

"You sound like an episode of *Dragnet*," he said, clearly amused. Then, as her lips tightened, he added hurriedly, "Okay, I apologize. And now that you've made your point, I was told to look for a redhead named Webster. Have I got the right one this time?"

"I'm Jessica Webster," she admitted reluctantly. "Is this Henry's idea?"

"You might say so." His critical surveillance matched the tone of his voice. "You're Tom Webster's sister, aren't you?"

"That's right." Jessica's eyebrows came together as she tried to remember if she'd ever seen him before their altercation on the ferry. Just as she was deciding that he definitely wasn't the type of man that she'd forget, a blast of a horn from an impatient driver behind the truck made her give a nervous start.

"C'mon—get in, will you?" He opened the door and reached for her luggage, shoving it onto the seat between them as she managed to scramble aboard. Hardly giving her time to put her tote bag on her lap and pull the door closed again, he made a left turn up the hill toward the main part of town. "I suppose you'll want to do some grocery shopping before you go out to the house."

"I guess so." Jessica hung on to her suitcase to keep her balance as the truck lurched through a pothole on the street. He was going too fast, she thought as she tried to sort out this newest angle. "Look," she managed to say when he finally braked in the middle of the block so that a tour group could cross to the other side of the street, "who are you?"

He turned for the briefest moment to meet her

questioning glance and then faced the front again. "Cal Sloane. I knew your brother when I was in college. And Henry," he added in a wry tone. "I knew he was here but I was surprised to find that Tom was providing a roof over his head and mine. At least, for the first week or so."

"You mean—you were staying at the house too?" Jessica asked, and had to clutch the door as the truck jerked forward again.

"Sorry. The transmission's shot on this thing."

"I'm not surprised." Jessica was resigned as he finally managed to find a parking place in front of a busy supermarket. "Henry isn't the mechanical type. If you get him away from a microscope, he's lost. Even so, he should take better care of his belongings."

"Oh, I don't think he owns this," Cal Sloane said with amusement.

"Who does?"

"Well—indirectly—I guess you do. Since you're taking Tom's place for the moment." He pulled the key out of the ignition and reached for his door handle. "I'll go in with you." Giving her a casual sideways glance, he added, "If it makes you feel any better, I spent a week and a half with Henry early on. Incidentally, he was sorry that he couldn't meet you but he'd made other plans. That's why I was pressed into service."

"I . . . I . . . don't understand. You mean you've talked to him this morning?"

"Nothing like that," he said impatiently, obviously waiting for her to precede him into the grocery. "He made the arrangement with me a couple of days ago before I went down to Seattle. Since he knew we'd be taking the same ferry."

Jessica hung back on the sidewalk, unaware that

she was causing a minor pedestrian traffic jam. "But your other car . . ." she said, her voice trailing off uncertainly.

"It's parked on the waterfront. I thought you'd better decide whether you wanted the truck for transportation while you're here"—he jerked his head at the vintage vehicle behind them— "or whether you'd want to make other arrangements."

"You seem to have been doing a lot of 'arranging' for me already," she told him in a tone of voice that showed she didn't appreciate it.

He shrugged. "Henry's idea. If you don't like it, you can have it out with him. S'matter of fact, I'd better drive you down by the Institute on the way. Damned if I know what he did with the house keys."

"You really don't need to bother about that," Jessica said, letting him propel her into the supermarket while she dug into her purse, finally pulling out a key ring triumphantly. "I have my own key right here."

Cal shook his head as he commandeered a wheeled cart for her groceries. "That won't do you any good. Henry had the locks changed just a couple weeks ago. The place resembles a fortress these days—dead bolts and all."

"He might have let me know." Jessica shoved the useless key back into her purse and took control of the shopping cart. "It wasn't too many years ago that they didn't even bother to lock the doors up here." Then, noting a shopper whose appearance showed that he'd evidently given up bathing along with other amenities of civilization, she added wryly, "Apparently things have changed."

"You'd better believe it. Look, I've a couple calls to make, and the closest public phone is at the corner.

I'll meet you at the checkout here when you've finished shopping. Okay?"

"Of course. Or I can just meet you in the truck,"
Jessica started to say, but let her voice drop when she
saw that he'd already turned away and was striding
toward the door. Obviously he wasn't the type who
spent his spare time trundling a cart around a grocery
store, she told herself as she turned down the nearest
aisle. Or if he did, he'd head for the gourmet section.
Not Henry's type at all, she thought with a small
frown, and tried to remember what her brother had
said about Cal Sloane.

She almost collided with a floor display of paper
towels as her memory suddenly returned. It wasn't
Cal Sloane in those days, but "Caleb," as Tom had
teasingly called him. Apparently his name was the
only thing even slightly old-fashioned about him, if
Tom's stories were to be believed. Caleb Sloane had
held the record for making the most of fraternity
social life in his undergraduate career, and then done
an abrupt about-face in his final college years. "His
folks were killed abroad—an avalanche during a skiing
holiday," Tom had reported one Thanksgiving vacation. "Now Cal has more money than he can spend
but he doesn't seem to give a damn. He's even planning on graduate school, for God's sake! Half the
women on Sorority Row have gone into mourning."

In retrospect, Jessica could very well believe it.
Aside from that overbearing attitude, he was the type
of man that any red-blooded woman would find im-
possible to ignore. Tall, lean, with measurements
that made his jeans look as if they'd been fitted by a
Savile Row tailor, while the cable-knit sweater only
served to emphasize the width of his shoulders.

The outer shell was deceptive, though, because

that gray-eyed glance of his speared anything that moved and his jaw was as formidable as the bow of the Washington State ferry down at the pier.

It was obvious, too, that she hadn't impressed him during their short acquaintance. Which put them on equal footing, she told herself emphatically as she reached for a quart of milk and deposited it in the shopping basket. Her schedule for the next week or so didn't allow for any dalliance and, considering the number of acquaintances she had in Texas, she didn't feel the need to nail any new masculine scalps to her front door. Probably the best way to get her point across was to drive him back to his car and send him on his way as soon as possible.

She was still considering that option when she saw Cal loom into view at the other end of the dairy case, and it took only a glance at his grim expression to realize that something had gone radically wrong.

He didn't waste any time in letting her know it. He lifted the quart of milk from her cart and put it back in the refrigerated case even as he took her elbow with his free hand. "You can skip that," he said brusquely, steering her toward the front entrance of the store. "Something's happened that's shot everything to hell!"

"I don't understand," she said, struggling to get free from his clasp. "And I wish you'd stop dragging me—"

"Pipe down, will you!"

Jessica noticed the curious glances from nearby shoppers and realized that her voice had risen as they went past the check stand. She swallowed and managed a thin smile as they walked out the front door and across the sidewalk. As soon as they reached the parked truck, however, she said through gritted teeth,

"This had damn well better be good! If you have the idea that I'm impressed by your caveman tactics, you have another think coming. Just because—"

"I tried to get in touch with Henry," Cal said, interrupting her ruthlessly.

"That's no excuse for—"

"He's been hurt," Cal continued as if she hadn't spoken.

His ominous pronouncement made Jessica draw in her breath and forget about her anger. "Oh, Lord! I didn't realize." She bit her lip as she stared up at him. "It's bad, isn't it?"

Cal's mouth compressed to a stern line. "At least he's still alive. They took him by helicopter to the burn center in Seattle about an hour or so ago, and the doctors sounded encouraging. The people he worked with at the Institute are pretty unstrung, though." Cal opened the truck door and motioned her in. "I'd like to drive down there now and talk to somebody who was on the scene. Somehow, I have the feeling there's more to the story than the receptionist was telling. If I can manage to see Henry's secretary, she might know more than the bare facts."

Jessica nodded, waiting until he'd closed her door and slid onto the driver's seat before she said hesitantly, "Maybe it would be better if I waited in the truck when we get there. There'll be enough confusion without my adding to it."

Cal said, "We'll see," in an absentminded tone as he reversed into the main street and, a little later, turned onto a road which Jessica remembered as one of the arterials out of town. She stayed quietly in her corner, automatically noting how the shops had moved out almost to the city limits in recent years. Prosperity, or at least a swelling of the population, was making a mark on the sleepy village.

Cal must have been on the same wavelength, because as they turned off the main road onto a gravel track after a mile or so, he said, "The Institute's really changed things in this part of the country. The good part is the creation of new jobs."

"And the bad part?" she asked when he didn't continue.

He turned his concentration from the road long enough to give her a wry smile. "The natives don't like change. You should know that. Tom said your family was here almost at the beginning."

Jessica gave an undignified snort. "You make it sound as if we sat round the campfire to smoke a peace pipe."

"Does that mean that you're not against change?"

"Not if it accompanies progress." She gestured toward the thick stand of timber on either side of the road. "It looks to me as if there's plenty of untouched property left, considering that we're only about five minutes out of town." Then, as the truck bounced roughly through potholes, she added, "S'matter of fact, I'm all for improving this road if that wouldn't upset the old guard."

"I'll go along with that," Cal said, braking as they encountered a stretch of washboard and the truck fishtailed on the loose gravel. "Although I don't think you can blame the highway department for this. Henry said it was a private road and the Institute doesn't want to encourage visitors."

"Well, they're going about it in the right way." Jessica clung to the door handle as they started down a steep hill. "Hey, look! There's a visitor in the parking lot now."

"Not four-wheeled but four-legged," Cal said with a grin as he drove carefully around a big raccoon who was leisurely making his way back into the undergrowth. Cal pulled the truck into an empty space at the end of the lot and turned off the engine before saying, "Sure you don't want to come in? There's a tidal-pool display down on the lower level that's Henry's pride and joy."

Jessica shook her head. "I'll wait until he's well again and can show it to me in person. Go ahead. I've a book in my purse, so I don't mind waiting."

"Okay. I shouldn't be too long," he said, getting out of the truck.

Jessica watched him disappear down a wide path toward a one-story administration building which was nicely designed to fit into the wooded landscape at the edge of the water. She was aware, too, that Cal Sloane seemed to fit the new surroundings almost like a chameleon. At that moment, he was quite different from the man she'd encountered on the ferry, and she wondered idly which identity was the real one. Henry could shed light on it, but there were far more important things in his life just then.

Jessica's glance wandered over the small structures that ranged on down the beach from one end of the main building. The Institute must have considerable funding to be that size. As she watched a supply truck unloading, she speculated on how many personnel it took to run the place. Strange how she'd imagined a much smaller installation when she'd read about it. Apparently Henry had found his right niche, after all. She chewed on her thumbnail, hoping that poor Henry's injuries weren't as serious as they had feared and that he'd be back at his beloved work soon.

She debated getting out of the truck and wandering around, but finally decided against it. Her lack of sleep was beginning to catch up with her and she rested her head against the worn vinyl seat, deciding that she'd take a full-fledged nap once she reached her grandmother's house, before deciding what to do with the rest of her day.

Weariness and the warm summer air made a mockery of her resolution because she was sound asleep when she heard the truck door open a little later. She struggled upright to see Cal settling behind the wheel. "Sorry," she muttered, and then yawned outright as she tried to gather her thoughts. "I didn't mean to doze off. Maybe I'm still on central time." When he didn't reply, she frowned and squinted, trying to get her sleep-dazed eyes to focus properly. "You look terrible," she blurted out then as she surveyed his face. "I mean—it must have been bad news. Henry's all right, isn't he? He didn't . . ." Her voice trailed off fearfully.

"Die?" Cal shook his head. "No. He'll be okay. Valerie had just gotten a report from the burn center and it was encouraging."

"That's wonderful!" Jessica said in relief. Then she asked, "Who's Valerie?"

"Henry's secretary. Valerie Long. She's the one I was talking to. You'll probably meet her if you stick around."

Even in Jessica's benumbed state, his last comment set off warning bells. "What do you mean—*if* I stick around? Why on earth wouldn't I?"

He rubbed the back of his neck as if his collar were too tight. Which was ridiculous, Jessica thought, since a crewneck sweater certainly wasn't uncomfortable.

His next words showed that his wardrobe wasn't

what was on his mind. "Because as of this morning," he told her, "there's no place for you to stay. The fire—the one that caused Henry's accident—was at your property." As she stared back at him, wide-eyed, as if unable to comprehend, he went on slowly. "The house. Your grandmother's house. I'm sorry, but apparently it's a total write-off. They're investigating the cause of it now."

2

As Jessica walked slowly up to the air terminal on the island a month and a half later, she was thinking how much could change in such a short time. On this trip, the colors of fall had predominated from her first glimpse of the island—even though parts of the landscape were hidden under elusive wisps of fog. It was a stubborn seasonal fog which had blanketed most of the western part of the state for several days and caused massive disruptions to the flight arrivals in Seattle and later had delayed her connection on the inter-island plane.

A gust of wind swirled the dust on the walk under her feet and made her shiver momentarily. Definitely fall weather, she thought, and felt an instant's longing for the sunny eighty degrees she'd left the night before in Dallas.

The Friday Harbor air terminal wasn't large but it reflected the newfound prosperity of the island, with its polished floor and sparkling glass windows. Before Jessica followed the other passengers to retrieve her baggage, she glanced out at the adjoining parking lot and raised her eyebrows at the the rows of expensive cars in the commuter area. Then, before she could turn back to the counter, an attractive woman standing by the door raised a hand to get her attention. "Miss Webster?"

"That's right." Jessica frowned slightly as she went over to her. "What's gone wrong now?"

The other woman uttered a low laugh and held out her hand. "Not a thing, so far as I know. I'm Valerie Long. I've talked to you on the phone."

"Henry's secretary, of course." Jessica noted that Valerie's handshake was firm and brisk, surprisingly at variance with her husky, provocative voice. Her thick dark hair was corralled neatly in one braid worn over her shoulder, giving her thin face a severity which lightened only with her fleeting smile. A dark cotton dress of mid-calf length and flat sandals were casual to the extreme and did little to flatter her figure. The only touch of elegance came from a pair of gold bow-knot earrings which looked expensive and beautiful.

Valerie must have been aware of her rapid survey because the smile flashed again. "I had to make a mad dash to be here on time. Your flight was postponed, but then, I don't have to remind you of that, do I?"

"Not really." Jessica shook her head ruefully. "I can tell you exactly how many flights were postponed or canceled. I spent most of the morning staring out at the Sea-Tac runway waiting for the fog to go away. Probably I should have taken the ferry."

"They've all been late too. Living on the island" —Valerie gestured expansively—"you get used to it. Is that your baggage on the cart?" she asked as the passengers suddenly descended at the end of the counter.

"I imagine so." Jessica held back to say, "I wanted to arrange for a taxi before I—"

"My dear, that's why I'm here." Valerie urged her gently toward the counter. "Cal thought you'd need transportation."

"Caleb Sloane?" Jessica pulled up short in amazement. "You mean he's still around?"

"At times." Valerie looked at her watch. "I don't want to rush you, but—"

"I'm sorry." Jessica was remembering that her arrival must have disrupted the secretary's work schedule, and she headed for the baggage counter again, saying over her shoulder, "I see mine on the end, so it won't take a minute."

"In that case, I'll bring the car around and meet you in front of the door," Valerie announced, her good humor restored. She continued a few minutes later when Jessica's cases had been stored in the trunk of a modest car with the Institute's official shield emblazoned on the side of it. "We'll head straight for your apartment," Valerie said, after Jessica had joined her on the front seat and closed her door. "Then I'll go on back to work."

"I have the feeling that I'm not only causing a lot of inconvenience but that this is illegal as well," Jessica said, gesturing toward a mail bag with the Institute seal on it which was between them on the floor.

"It's just a small detour, and Henry felt it was the least we could do."

"I thought you said Cal Sloane," Jessica began, only to have Valerie interrupt.

"Well, he was in on it too. But Henry called again this morning from the hospital to make sure that everything was all set for you. Really, that man is running up the most astronomical long-distance charges. It's a good thing he has a private phone by his bed."

"I'm just glad that he's well enough to be taking an interest in things," Jessica said, absently noting the attractive fall colors of the trees which lined the service road to the airport before the secretary turned onto the main highway.

Valerie nodded. "He said that you'd kept in touch. It meant a lot to him, especially since he felt so guilty about the destruction of your house."

"I don't know why." Jessica kept her voice carefully level. "He certainly wasn't the arsonist."

"You haven't even been out to see the place, have you? Or what's left of the foundation?"

For a moment Jessica resented the other's casual tone, and then common sense triumphed. After all, it was just another happening to Valerie Long. An old house had been destroyed and she couldn't possibly be aware of how many memories had gone up in smoke with it. Jessica kept her gaze on the curving two-lane road ahead of them as she said, "No. There wasn't time. I went back to Seattle to make sure that Henry was all right in the hospital, and then I had an emergency summons from my boss back in Texas."

"You were gone for quite a while."

"There were some departmental changes. I'm in public relations and our biggest account suddenly needed a new approach to the corporate image."

"I know what that means." Valerie sounded more sympathetic than she had before. "Keeping the right image for the public means a great deal to the Institute too. Our directors fuss about it all the time. Especially when it's time for new budget proposals." She braked slightly as a pickup threatened them from a side road, and then accelerated again. "Cal took you down to see Henry?"

"Well, we went to Seattle on the same afternoon flight. I haven't seen him since," Jessica said trying to disguise her annoyance at Cal Sloane's quick disappearance that day and the fact that she hadn't heard boo from him in the interim. Not that she really expected to, or even wanted to, for heaven's sake.

"Does my driving bother you?" Valerie asked, turning to face her for an instant.

"No." Jessica looked blankly back at her. "Why?"

"You looked so unhappy for a minute. I thought maybe this island traffic was getting to you." Valerie changed lanes to pass a car which was double-parked with the flashers on.

Jessica chuckled, thinking of the comparison with the traffic she'd encountered en route to the Dallas-Fort Worth airport. "San Juan roads are pure paradise compared with where I live these days."

"Then it was something else. What were we talking about? Oh, yes. Cal's disappearance. You mustn't feel hurt." Valerie chattered on. "He's the most elusive man I've ever met. One week, he was dropping in my office every day, but he still tried to uphold that 'elusive-male' role. Not that it was necessary. Some women aren't interested in a permanent relationship either." She spared a self-satisfied glance at her reflection in the rearview mirror before adding, "I told him so at the very beginning."

Valerie was conducting a two-level conversation, Jessica decided. Her spoken words were deliberately innocuous but she managed to plant the impression that Caleb Sloane had been dancing attendance on her until she'd laid out the ground rules. Her pleased expression when she mentioned his name showed that it wouldn't take much persuasion from him to make her bend the rules accordingly.

"I don't suppose you'll be on the island long," Valerie said as they approached the beginning of the small business district. "Henry said something about your planning to sell the property—it sounds like the sensible thing to do under the circumstances."

"I really haven't made up my mind." Jessica kept her voice carefully bland, deciding that Valerie wasn't going to learn anything from her. It sounded like the secretary could compete with native tom-toms in dispensing local gossip, so it was a good thing that Henry was doing whale research instead of high-tech on Silicon Row. "The brown and yellow colors are really beautiful at this season, aren't they? So different from summer with the green conifers."

Jessica's deliberate change of subject wasn't appreciated. She could see that in the tightening of Valerie's lips. "Didn't you know? Scenery is the island's main claim to fame," the secretary said sarcastically. She took her hand from the steering wheel to gesture at the three blocks which comprised the center of town. "There's certainly not much else here to get excited about—and this is the good season."

"I gather you'd rather be somewhere else," Jessica said, deciding to do a little probing of her own.

"Not really. I adore my work at the Institute—it's so worthwhile."

Her hushed tone was impressive but Jessica was tempted to point out that even Henry's splendid research on marine life really wasn't a matter of life or death. Except his. That fact made her ask casually, "Henry still seems pretty foggy about the injuries he sustained."

Valerie had to brake at an intersection to let a

group of teenagers cross the street, and she turned to frown at Jessica. "That's not surprising—considering how badly he was burned."

"I know. But I wonder why he risked going in the burning house at all. After all, if he hadn't made that trip back to his office to check some data, he might have been in the house when the fire was set. No one would have blamed him if he'd just stayed out on the front lawn after he came back, and watched it burn."

"I'm surprised that you take that attitude—since he was trying to protect *your* property," Valerie said with some asperity.

"I would have preferred it if he'd emerged unscathed and kept out of the hospital." Jessica watched her turn off the main street and, after a block or so, drive down another steep road. "At least he's making a wonderful recovery and should be back to work in a few weeks."

"I know. That's what he told me the last time he called," Valerie informed her, as if determined to set the record straight. She pulled the car into a vacant stall in a long carport which was almost at the water's edge and very close to the town's ferry terminal. As Jessica got out of the car, she saw one of the big green-and-white ferries emerge from a patch of fog out on the water and slowly maneuver in the channel to approach the pier.

Then she glanced up at the complex of low buildings along the shore to her right and turned a puzzled face to Valerie, who had slid out from behind the wheel. "Why did we stop here?"

The secretary shifted her thick braid of hair on her shoulder in an automatic gesture. "This is where you're staying. Didn't you know?"

"Here?" Jessica looked around in bewilderment. "I didn't see any signs."

"It's not a hotel." Valerie's tone was indulgent. "They're condos. This is one of the nicest spots on the island, so you can thank your stars that you can stay here. It's the first time I've ever heard of a short-term rental. I'll help with the garment bag if you can hand it out." She gestured toward the back of the car.

"My what? Oh!" Jessica turned back and hauled her things out. "Thanks very much."

Valerie didn't waste any time after that, leading the way down a concrete path behind the buildings, where neatly tended gardens provided a blaze of color for the back entrances to the apartments. A few of the porches had bikes alongside, together with scuba gear stacked in neat piles.

The secretary didn't comment on them, simply striding ahead in her brisk way and finally turning up a short stairway at the second building in the complex. Jessica lingered long enough to notice there was a postage-stamp bit of lawn and an elevated border of marigolds and purple petunias above the long narrow pier that rimmed the water. In front of it there were a dozen or so slips with power boats and a large sailboat tied to them. The gently bobbing boats together with the forested hills edging the water across the cove provided a spectacular scene.

"Aren't you coming?"

Valerie's impatient comment from the open porch above made Jessica hurry up the steps. "Sorry," she said breathlessly when she arrived at the front door. "It's so pretty here. It's like rediscovering treasure when I come back."

"Umm."

Valerie's murmur, though noncommittal, showed what she thought of that. Jessica grimaced and apologized again. "I didn't mean to delay you."

"Well, I really should get back to the office." Valerie had fished out a key and unlocked the door, gesturing Jessica inside. "You'll have plenty of time to look at the view—especially without a car. I suppose you'll rent one for the short time you're here."

Jessica thought about mentioning the truck and then decided not to, since she didn't even know where it was. "Probably," she agreed in an offhand manner. After shoving her bag in the compact foyer, she wandered into the living area with its floor-to-ceiling windows. "This *is* nice!"

"Certainly one of the best views in town," Valerie agreed, following her in after depositing the garment bag atop the suitcase. "The furnishings are all right too—if you like gold and brown."

Which she presumably didn't, Jessica thought. Personally, she thought the beige-and-brown linen couch and upholstered chairs looked both comfortable and attractive. There was also a Roman brick fireplace and dull gold carpet to add the illusion of warmth to the room. An adjoining contemporary dining area with teak furniture led into a small but efficient kitchen.

She decided to explore further while Valerie was investigating the contents of the kitchen cabinets, and found a functional utility room plus two bedrooms with attached baths.

"You certainly will have enough room." Valerie had come up behind her to peer into the master bedroom with its big double bed and upholstered headboard. "I can't imagine how Henry pulled enough strings to get this rental. He certainly didn't mention it before, and we had some really important members of the state legislature up at the Institute this fall. We're hoping to get some additional funding," she explained, realizing that her comment hadn't been exactly diplomatic.

Jessica shrugged and walked back out to the kitchen to investigate the cupboards. "I'm certainly not going to ask questions about how it came about. I'll just enjoy it."

Valerie's eyebrows went up. "You know what they say about Greeks bearing gifts."

"Anyone who knows Henry certainly realizes that he doesn't work that way," Jessica said crisply. "I wonder who stocked up on groceries. At least I can offer you some tea or coffee—there are all sorts of staples in here."

"So I noticed." Valerie pushed her braid back again with an impatient gesture as she slid the strap of her purse onto her shoulder. "I can't spare any more time. I've left my phone number at work." She gestured toward a slip of paper on the counter near the sink. "If you have problems, I'll do what I can."

"That's thoughtful of you." Jessica was able to infuse a little more sincerity into her tone than Valerie had managed, and went over to hold the door for her. "I'll try not to bother you. I think I'll need that," she added, holding out her palm.

Valerie stared at her and then realized that Jessica was talking about the door key she'd just dropped into her purse. "Oh!" She managed an apologetic grimace as she handed it over. "I just presumed that Henry had given you one earlier."

Jessica smiled back. "No problem," she said, putting it on the counter and resisting the urge to ask the secretary why she should keep a key to the apartment as well. "Thanks again for meeting me at the airport."

She watched Henry's secretary trip down the path and then closed the front door carefully, leaning against it with a sigh of relief. At least she'd managed to see the woman off the premises without actually coming to blows. She shook her head slightly as she thought about it. Valerie was attractive if you liked the "earth-mother" garb and assertive manner. Probably she had Henry completely cowed, but it was strange that Cal Sloane was one of her followers. Two such dominant personalities would be apt to crash head-on. Unless Valerie changed her tactics when dealing with an available man.

Jessica straightened then, annoyed that she was letting her imagination run riot. Why on earth did it matter? She'd have a quick cup of tea and then wander uptown and see about renting a car. There was a garage just a few blocks away that should be able to supply her needs. She'd find out what had happened to the truck some other time—it wasn't worth any exhaustive inquiries at the moment. If she started phoning round, Cal might think she was trying to renew their acquaintance. A happening not even to be considered, she told herself firmly.

It wasn't much later that she was thanking her stars she'd been sensible—for a change. She'd had her cup of tea and hung some things in the closet before setting out the few blocks to the main street of town. There weren't as many people on the sidewalk as earlier in the season. Most of the population could be seen in the two supermarkets purchasing groceries for their evening meal. Jessica decided to eat out, since she wasn't in the mood for any serious cooking, and the prospect of a frozen dinner was unappealing.

After arranging for the car rental, she'd try one of the attractive restaurants at the water's edge.

She was practically at the end of the block when two men came out of a real-estate office and almost bumped into her on the sidewalk. Jessica sidestepped rapidly to avoid the collision and started to make a cheerful comment, when she noticed who was holding her elbow to make sure that she'd regained her balance.

"I'm sorry," Cal Sloane said, moving back a step when he saw that she was safely upright. "We should have been looking where we were going."

"I don't know about that." His companion, who was a genial man in his early forties, cut in without ceremony. "It's the best thing that's happened to me all day. I'm Bruce Lightner," he told Jessica, and gestured to the name on his office window. "I don't usually knock down my prospective customers, Miss . . ." He paused suggestively.

Jessica's glance flew to Cal, but he clearly wasn't going to perform any introductions. "Just a weekend tourist passing by, Mr. Lightner," she told the stocky real-estate man politely. "And I was not coming in. At least, not this time."

"Doesn't matter, I hope there was no harm done," the older man replied in genial fashion.

"Not at all—I'm perfectly fine, thanks," she told him, still seething at Cal's decision to treat her like a stranger. "Now, if you'll excuse me . . ."

She started down the sidewalk but was still within earshot when she heard Bruce Lightner say to Cal, "You were a little slow on the uptake there, man. My generation had better reflexes when we bumped into a gorgeous lady."

Jessica didn't dare glance over her shoulder to see

what happened after that. Probably Cal had turned his back on her anyhow. Damn that man!

She was unaware that she'd said it aloud until the man tending the gas pump at the garage gave her a startled look. "Something you needed, miss?" he asked tentatively.

"I want to rent a car," Jessica told him, and then softened her demand with a smile. "I need a way to get around while I'm on the island. Can you help me?"

"Most people arrange for rentals at the airport, but we've got one in here today. I just finished servicing it." He gestured toward a mid-size blue car parked at the side of the station. "Would that be okay?"

"It looks like just what I wanted." Jessica fished in her purse for her credit card and followed him into the building to complete the paperwork. "This must be my lucky day, after all."

Ten minutes later she was driving down the main street, pleased that the transportation problem was solved so easily. She slowed as she came to the intersection near the parking lot for her condominium and then deliberately turned the other way. She was strangely restless and had no desire to go back and sit in the empty apartment—no matter how attractive the surroundings. What she should do was go out and view the remains of her family's burned-out house so that she could make an intelligent decision about putting the property on the market. Definitely what she should do, she told herself, and then turned at the next intersection to drive past the restaurants at the waterfront. If she had an early dinner, she wasn't apt to run into Cal and his friend again. Not only that—a decent dinner would improve her mood.

It wasn't surprising she was feeling low, she told herself as she slowed to survey the almost empty parking lot of a restaurant close by the ferry slip and then turned into it. Food was all she needed to feel halfway human again.

She walked into the restaurant foyer and lingered by the cashier's desk, ostensibly to read the menu but actually to survey the scattered patrons. She gave a sigh of relief when she didn't recognize a soul, and allowed the hostess to lead her to a small table by the window.

The view was spectacular, although fragments of fog were starting to settle over the water out in the channel. "That means the ferries will be running late again," sighed the waitress as she brought Jessica a cup of coffee while she waited for her salmon entrée. "That's been going on all week. The schedule gets slower and slower at this season. It's murder if you commute to the mainland."

Jessica gave her a sympathetic smile but decided that the ferry schedules weren't the only thing on a slow-down schedule. Her suspicions were confirmed when her dinner was finally delivered with an apology.

"It's our new chef," the waitress said, putting down the plate in front of her. As Jessica looked dubiously at the charred edges of the fish, the woman said, "I could get you something else—but it'll take a while."

Jessica picked up her fork. "Never mind. I'm sort of in a hurry."

The waitress nodded apologetically. "I'll bring you some rolls and hot coffee. He didn't have anything to do with them."

Even by just eating half of her dinner and skipping dessert, darkness was starting to fall when Jessica went out to her car again. Her lips quirked as she surveyed the almost empty parking lot as she drove off. She needn't have worried about running into Cal or his real-estate friend. Probably the news about the new restaurant cook had spread quickly among the natives and they wouldn't show until the food improved.

The twilight scene was a quiet one as she drove through the business section and found herself on the familiar road which led toward her family's property at the far end of the island. At the rate darkness was falling, she'd just have time for a quick look around before light disappeared.

And maybe that was the easiest way, she thought soberly as she increased her speed on the deserted two-lane road. The advancing darkness would soften some of the horror of the burned remains, like a filter on a camera lens could hide the imperfections of a fading actress. Tomorrow, in the cold light of day, Jessica told herself, she'd gird herself to make the final decision on selling.

She hadn't realized it would be so hard. The island's autumn beauty was insidious. Like the evening fog which was settling in little patches over the lush meadows and in the tops of the russet-colored maples—it seemed to play at providing light accent touches to the landscape before settling with a vengeance during the night.

That realization made Jessica press down a little harder on the accelerator. She had no wish to be stranded on her return to town and it was entirely possible, the way the weather looked.

It was just ten minutes later that she turned down the road leading to English Camp, which adjoined her family's property. The Park Service entrance was always kept in first-class condition and was bound to be in better condition than the steep driveway leading down to the family place. She'd park her car in the public lot and walk down to the water, approaching the burned-out house from the beach.

Fortunately, the fog hadn't worsened by the time she parked in the big deserted area and got out of the car. She glanced around and shivered instinctively, realizing for the first time that she was very much alone. Then, giving herself a mental jab for letting her imagination run rampant, she briskly locked the car and dropped the keys in her purse before setting out down the wide steep trail to the beach.

It was lined on either side by maples, and other than her shoes scuffing along the fine gravel surface, there was only the barely discernible sound of leaves drifting down through the still evening air.

Jessica pulled up to watch for a minute, surprised to find that leaves *did* make a noise—landing on the path with a soft crisp sound which wouldn't have been noticed if there had been any other distraction.

At that moment, a shore bird keened mournfully overhead and she pulled up again, shivering as she crossed her arms over her breast. Maybe it would be best to give up this solitary communing with nature and come back in the morning like most people.

"No way!" she told herself then. It was a matter of principle. Only an idiot would drive all that way and then give up a few hundred yards from her destination.

She increased her pace down the path, able to see the water lapping at the slight bank ahead of her just beyond the velvety green expanse of park lawn. Turning left at a monster tree, she saw the waist-high picket fence which marked the site where English soldiers had planted a garden even before they'd constructed a barracks so many years ago. The Park

Department had faithfully tried to maintain a replica, and there was still some color in the well-defined flowerbeds, despite the lateness of the season. Beyond the garden area ran the fence that marked the boundary of the public area and the start of her family's holdings.

Almost fearfully, her glance went from the gentle slope to the dock at the waterside. At least the pier was undamaged, she noticed as she walked around the picket fence toward her destination. It wasn't surprising—there was certainly no reason to try to destroy an ancient dock that really wasn't very big.

She frowned then and her eyes narrowed as she peered through the darkening scene. Was there movement from that piece of driftwood at the edge of the beach? Surely there wasn't enough current to move any piece that big. Her glance swiftly swept the water of the cove, confirming that it was mirror-calm. Slowly, then, she unhooked the boundary gate and went through onto her family's property, keeping a steady gaze on the obstruction half in and half out of the water, where something was afloat and moving just enough to attract her attention.

Another two steps and she drew to a halt, bending forward to make a cautious identification. Then she drew in a horrified breath and ran the rest of the way to the water's edge—sliding onto her knees beside Cal Sloane's inert form.

"My God!" She ran a frantic hand over his face and bent down to confirm that he *was* breathing. "Cal!" she implored breathlessly, willing him to open his eyes and then moaning, "Oh, Lord!" as her fingers encountered a lump behind his ear, which was undoubtedly responsible for his unconscious condition.

"You have to get out of the water," she said,

knowing that he couldn't hear a word she said but somehow feeling better pretending to communicate. She tried to support his head as she reached under his shoulders and dragged him a few feet up onto the bank. At least he was out of that icy water, she thought, going down on her knees again as she tried to recover from the effort of moving him.

The worst part was the fact that it was almost dark and he was in no condition to be left while she went for help. She leaned over and placed her face against his cold cheek, trying to impart what little warmth she could. "Cal . . . wake up! Please! I don't know what to do."

There was a slight movement beneath her. "For a start, you can turn off the tears." Cal's voice was thready, but it gained strength as he went on. "I sure as hell don't need any more water on me." He managed to shove up on an elbow then and surveyed her dispassionately. "And what in the devil are you doing out here anyhow?"

3

Jessica stared at him wide-eyed before snarling, "So you recognize me this time? I'm surprised that you didn't cut me dead again." Then remorse replaced her flare of temper as she saw him doggedly trying to sit erect. "Oh, Lord! I'm sorry. I was so scared—"

"I know. You didn't know whether to kill me or kiss me," he finished for her. His voice was almost back to normal but his face looked pinched with cold. As he glanced at the wavelets lapping on the shore below them, he added, "I didn't help matters. I knew I had to get out of there but I hadn't gathered enough strength until you appeared." Then he frowned as another thought occurred. "It's almost dark. Did you bring a flashlight with you?"

"No. I was just making a quick trip. But if I leave now, I can reach the parking lot and go for help. You can have my jacket, and if you can shelter against one of the tree trunks out of the wind—"

"Forget it," Cal said, cutting into her orders. "I'm not staying here."

His tone didn't invite any further discussion, but Jessica protested even as she helped him to his feet.

"You'll never make it up that trail to the parking lot. It's a challenge even if you're in good condition."

"Which I'm not," he agreed, and clutched her shoulder for support. "Sorry, I didn't mean to hurt you." He let his hand slide off as he saw her wince.

"Don't be silly." Jessica made up her mind in an instant and put an arm around his waist. "Hang onto me—anyplace you can. If we get over to the park buildings, there's bound to be more shelter than out here in the open. Maybe I can even break into one so you'll be away from the cold."

"That won't be necessary," Cal told her through a tight jaw as they lurched back toward the park boundary. "I parked my car down on the lower level of the staff lot."

"You're in no condition to drive anywhere."

"We finally agree on something," he said whimsically. "I hoped that you'd do the honors and take me back to town." When she hesitated he went on, "*If* it doesn't interfere with your plans for the evening."

"Don't be an idiot! My social schedule is nonexistent." She glared up at his pale face, which was so close to her shoulder as he clung to her for support. "I just was wondering if we shouldn't switch to my car." Then, seeing the struggle he was having to even walk beside her, she said, "It doesn't matter. The important thing now is just to get to a car."

"We even agree on the priorities. This must be a first—"

She cut in. "And you'd do well to save your strength. Otherwise I'll be forced to drag you feet-first." As he gave an unwilling snort of laughter, she went on demurely, "That wouldn't do a thing for your ego."

Cal must have recognized the sense of her statement because he fell silent after that. Later, Jessica was to wonder how long that laborious struggle had taken them. By the time they reached the buildings of English Camp, darkness had fallen completely.

Cold fronds of fog hung above the scattered frame buildings, adding to the eerie scene. If it hadn't been for the dim light of the moon as it worked its way in and out of the cloud cover, they probably would have had to give up. As it was, they fell on one grassy hummock and, a few minutes later, almost stumbled as they collided with a Park Service descriptive marker in the middle of the field near the blockhouse.

"I know where we are now," Cal said slowly, as if every word were an effort. "My car's just over there." He gestured to the right and Jessica obediently turned in that direction. "My keys are still in my pocket, thank God," he said, fumbling in his trousers. "You'd better hang on to them."

She nodded and took the keys from him, deciding that it was best to keep conversation at a bare minimum until she could get him to the emergency room of a hospital.

The last fifty feet of their trek were the longest, and Jessica's fingers seemed all thumbs as she tried to unlock the car door. Cal pushed her aside to pull it open, and literally fell onto the front seat. He looked up as Jessica hovered uncertainly beside him. "It's okay—we made it."

"A tough fight, Mom—but we won," she quoted, hoping that the darkness hid the tears of relief that were sliding down her cheeks. "Can you close the door?"

"No problem." He reached for the handle. "I won't be sorry to see the last of this place."

But when Jessica slid behind the steering wheel a moment or so later, she found that she needn't have worried about mopping her cheeks. Rather than paying attention to her, Cal's gaze was focused on the water's edge.

"What are you looking at?" she asked before switching on the ignition.

"I thought I saw some running lights in the channel, but there's nothing there now. It might not hurt to hang around for a few minutes."

"No way." There wasn't any indecision in her tone as she started the engine. "I don't know what's behind all this, but you're not in condition for hand-to-hand combat at the moment. The only person I'm going to look for is somebody wearing a white coat."

He sat up a little straighter in the seat as she accelerated up the rough track toward the main park entrance at the top of the slope. "You mean a doctor?" When she remained obdurately silent, he growled, "If you think I'm going to stick around some hospital for the rest of the night, you're crazy!"

"I don't know why I worry," she replied in saccharine tones. "You certainly sound just the same." Pausing an instant for emphasis, she went on, "Your disposition hasn't changed one iota—it's just as unpleasant as always, and you're right about seeing the doctor."

"Of course I am."

"Because it would take a minor miracle to change that," she continued calmly, ignoring his interruption. "I don't think they could manage it in the emergency ward tonight."

There was a thick silence in the car after that until they reached the main road and Jessica turned back toward town, accelerating as fast as she dared when the patches of fog thinned. She cast an apprehensive glance toward the man slumped at her side then and felt a pang of remorse. There was no need for her to sound like a termagant when he was too weak to defend himself. At least he wouldn't know how much of her temper flare-up had been due to relief—she'd been scared stiff that he'd collapse halfway to the car.

"I'm sorry." Cal's voice sounded deeper than usual and he was taking care with his words, but there was no disguising the underlying sincerity of his tone. "It occurs to me that I haven't even thanked you for dragging me out of the water. And considering the fact that I cut you dead in town this afternoon, you couldn't have been blamed if you'd . . ." He paused, searching for the proper words.

". . . rolled you down into deep water," she supplied, her own voice unsteady with sudden relief.

He gave a snort of laughter and then stopped abruptly to touch the side of his head. "Ouch! One thing I'd better learn—no sudden movements for a while. There's a platoon of little men with hobnailed boots stomping around in my head just like the television commercials. It doesn't help to stir them up."

"Exactly why I'm driving to the emergency room of the local hospital. You probably have a mild concussion."

"Forget it. It isn't worth bothering about."

She gave him a brief sideways glance before turning her attention to the road again. "You're not going to win this one, Mr. Sloane, so you might as well relax. If the doctor or nurse or whoever gives you a clean bill of health, I'll drive you home. Although I'd think you'd prefer to stay around and let a pretty nurse soothe your fevered brow."

"Some other time." He sounded as if he really

didn't think it was worth the effort to argue any longer. "Okay. I'll let them run the yardstick over me, but I'm not signing in any hospital. There's too much at stake right now."

"I don't understand." Unconsciously her foot let up on the gas pedal and the car's speed dropped as her puzzled gaze rested on his profile for another moment. "You mean that there's some mystery about all this? I thought that you'd fallen there on the beach."

His disgusted snort told her what his reaction was to that kind of logic, but he merely said in a tired tone, "Let's skip it. I'm not in the mood to explain now. Maybe later."

And it bloody well will be later, Jessica vowed silently as she increased the car's speed again. Cal Sloane might think that he was going to keep things to himself, but after the doctor took a look at him, she'd find out the truth once and for all.

There wasn't any more conversation until they reached the outskirts of town and she turned in at the one-story rambling structure that housed the local hospital. "I imagine there won't be any wait, since the summer season is over. The natives are a pretty healthy bunch," Jessica said lightly as they reached the curved drive which led to the emergency entrance. After she'd braked and turned off the ignition, she added, "Just stay put until I find someone."

"I'm perfectly able to walk—"

"Sit!"

"You make me feel like a French poodle," he complained, but stayed in the car as she slid out from behind the wheel.

"Wrong breed." She lingered to bestow a crooked smile. "Make it a St. Bernard."

"Don't forget—St. Bernards have teeth."

"In that case, I'll tell the doctor to bring a keg of brandy with him," she said over her shoulder, and marched into the building.

It took over an hour before the final verdict came in, but Cal finally had his way and was allowed to leave. By then, the lump behind his ear wasn't any smaller but at least the graze was clean and Jessica carried an envelope of pills to help him ease the pain.

"I told you there wasn't any concussion," he said triumphantly to her as he got back into the car again.

"Probably because you're so hardheaded." she replied, settling beside him with a flounce. The doctor said you were crazy not to stay in bed overnight."

"I have every intention of spending the night in bed. But not in that hospital," Cal said, spacing his words for emphasis.

"Very funny." A sudden thought struck her as she reached to turn on the ignition, and she shifted to face him. "Where *are* you going to spend the night? I don't even know where you live."

He slid down in the seat so that he could rest his head against the back of it. "Actually, in that same wing of condos where you're staying. The manager found a sublet for Henry and me after the fire."

Jessica frowned, noting absently that while Cal's voice was firmer than before, there was an underlying weariness that he couldn't disguise. "I don't think you should be alone there tonight," she said finally as they turned out of the hospital drive onto the road to the center of town.

"You can always check on me every four hours if you want to climb another flight of stairs. I'll leave the front door unlocked," he told her, and then had second thoughts. "No, it might be better if I gave you an extra key."

"Considering what happened earlier . . ." she said, probing gently.

"Umm. Something like that."

Which meant that he wasn't planning to start baring his soul, Jessica thought, and her lips tightened with annoyance. The man was even more stubborn than she had thought. If he hadn't already been bruised and battered, she would have been tempted to give him another lump.

"Don't even think of it." At her startled sideways glance, he went on, "You're make a terrible poker player—that face of yours is almost too easy to read." He yawned then, before adding, "We can have the great confessional later. Right now, that medicine the doctor gave me is raising hell with all my good intentions."

"For heaven's sake, don't fall asleep before we get to the apartment," she cautioned, accelerating down the deserted main street of town once they'd cleared the intersection. "It isn't much further."

Fortunately he was still awake when she pulled into a covered parking stall a little later. Patches of fog dimmed the lights atop the ferry landing area to the left, and somewhere nearby a metal halyard was striking rhythmically when the currents swelled.

Cal pushed open the gate to the condo entrance, hesitating just long enough to let Jessica through before closing it carefully behind him. He glanced out over the water then and said, "The fog gives the ferry pier an eerie look, doesn't it? I hadn't noticed it before tonight."

"Probably because you're prejudiced against anything to do with water at the moment," Jessica said calmly, setting a pace that he could manage in his weary state. "You'll feel better when you shed those damp clothes and get into something warm and dry. What's the matter?" she asked in some alarm as he pulled up and muttered a word under his breath.

"I forgot to call and have the electricity turned on when I moved into Henry's place this morning."

"You mean it's been turned off?" she asked, unbelieving.

"You know Henry," he said with resignation. "He's loath to part with any coin of the realm if it can be avoided. But this isn't his fault—I just plain forgot."

"It can be fixed tomorrow," Jessica said. "In the meantime, there's a perfectly good extra bedroom where I'm staying."

He started walking again after giving her a searching look. "If you're sure . . ."

"Absolutely. Besides, I'd have you on my conscience forever if you perished because I missed one of my four-hour checks during the night," she told him lightly. "We turn left at this path." She steered him in the proper direction. "If you can climb those few stairs, I'm at the apartment on the end."

Cal went doggedly up, although he needed the railing to make the last steps, and didn't say any more until she'd unlocked the apartment door and switched on the lights. "Thank God, it's warm in here!" he announced then as he leaned against the end of the kitchen counter.

Jessica gestured toward the nearby bath and opened the door to the room opposite. "There's an electric blanket on your bed. Together with a hot bath—you should feel better." A sudden thought occurred to her. "What about pajamas?"

He smiled slightly and fished a key ring out of his

pocket, separating one from the bunch. "Henry's apartment is on the upper deck—almost above this. There's a brown leather carry-on bag in the hall if you wouldn't mind doing the honors. I'm afraid that if I tried it right now . . ."

"You'd fall flat on your face," she finished for him, and took the key. "Try a hot bath instead." She lingered by the front door to give him a perturbed glance. "You *can* manage that, can't you?"

A wry grin lightened his face momentarily. "If I'm not out by the time you come back, you might sling in a life preserver. Of course, there's always mouth-to-mouth resuscitation."

"You're feeling better," she said, announcing it with some satisfaction. "Don't expect any more than the life preserver."

She was sure that she heard a chuckle as she closed the apartment door behind her. Her lips twitched as she thought about the exchange, amazed to find that Cal could indulge in lighthearted banter when he was obviously hurting from the top of his head to his toes.

It was still quiet as she moved toward the short flight of stairs which led from her deck to the upper level of condos. The boats tied up to the pier in front of the building were dark and apparently deserted. Only the narrow borders of light around the closed apartment curtains indicated that there were people anywhere in residence. Probably they were used to the fog hanging down over the dark water, she thought, and wondered why such things had never bothered her when she'd come to the island on family outings years before.

She shook her head at such foolish imaginings and marched steadily up to the door of the apartment which Henry was apparently subletting. Even as she unlocked it and pushed it slightly ajar, she could feel the cool, stale air that flowed outward. Hesitating just a moment longer before she stepped inside and fumbled for the light switch, she thought again how she'd made the right decision in having Cal stay in her apartment. Henry's apartment felt like the inside of an oyster, and then, as she flipped the switch up and down without any result, she shook her head in disgust. Of course! There wasn't any electricity—exactly as Cal had said. No heat, no light, no nothing. And unless she wanted to find his clothes by braille, she'd have to go down and bring back a flashlight.

As she stood hesitating in the doorway, there was a muffled thud from somewhere in the apartment. Jessica skittered nervously back out onto the porch. The dim light bordering the stairs showed that there wasn't anything around outside, and she sighed in relief as she started back down to her apartment to find a flashlight.

She was almost at her front door before she remembered that she'd left Henry's apartment door wide open, and then she shrugged. It couldn't get any colder in that place than it already was, so it wasn't a major crime.

A sound of muffled splashing came from behind the closed bathroom door as she let herself quietly into her apartment and tiptoed into the kitchen. Fortunately, she found a flashlight in the second drawer she opened, and she was back out on the stairs before she lost her nerve completely.

There wasn't any noise when she reached Henry's front door for the second time. She directed the beam of the flashlight into the living room as she lingered on the threshold, and then drew in a sharp breath at what the light revealed.

The furnishings in the studio apartment had been shoved around, with a chair overturned and the contents of one kitchen cupboard strewn untidily along the counter. Jessica flashed the light all over the room and then moved over to peer nervously into the bathroom, checking that it was deserted as well. Only when she was sure that the intruder or intruders had fled did she go back and lock the front door behind her to make sure they couldn't return and pay her an unexpected visit.

The contents of Cal's suitcase had suffered with the rest of the furnishings. Clothes were strewn around the carpet in the entranceway, and she took extra time to fold them back in the case trying to restore them in proper order.

There was a pair of dark green pajamas that had been pulled from a plastic bag, and leather slippers still in knit shoe socks were lying by the door. The contents of Cal's toiletry bag had been rifled as well, and it took another minute to put those things back in place, as well. On picking up a plastic container of after-shave, she tightened the top and then shrugged as she dropped it into the bag. Funny, she could have sworn that it would be loose. Perhaps the intruder had checked it out and spilled some before discarding it. Certainly there was a whiff of fragrance still lingering, although the cold air had dissipated most of it since her arrival.

She glanced over her shoulder nervously once again and then closed the case. A final look around the apartment took another instant before she opened the door and glanced down to make sure that the stairs and walkway were deserted. Then she shoved the suitcase outside and locked the apartment before making her way back to the lower level. The light from her living room, which spilled out onto the walkway, was a welcome sight as she approached.

She had no sooner opened the front door and switched off the flashlight than the door of the bathroom opened and Cal emerged, naked except for a bath towel knotted around his hips. He looked startled for an instant and then leaned against the door frame, saying, "You took longer than I thought—I was about to give up on the pajamas."

Jessica reminded herself that she'd seen far more masculine flesh on a southern California beach, and kept her tone as casual as his. "Evidently you finally got warm," she said, letting her glance roam over him.

For an instant she thought that his cheeks reddened and then decided she was imagining things as he said, "There wasn't much choice." He jerked his head toward the bathroom behind him. "Those pajamas hanging on the door were a little small, and pale pink isn't a favorite of mine."

"I'll remember." Jessica picked up his case and handed it to him. "How do you feel about dark green ones?"

He grinned and walked into the bedroom she'd allotted him, dropping the case casually on the bedspread. "Thanks very much. At least they're a step in the right direction."

Jessica hovered in the doorway long enough to ask, "Have you switched on the blanket yet?"

"I hadn't planned on turning in quite so soon," he commented even as he reached over to flip the dial on the bed table. "As soon as I get these pajamas on, I'll clean up the bathroom."

"Don't worry, I'll do that eventually," Jessica said as she started to close the door. "I'll come back in a minute with something to drink. Which do you prefer—cocoa or hot milk?"

"Hot milk! Good God! I haven't had that since I was seven years old."

"Then you'll be glad to know that it hasn't changed," she said in dulcet tones, and managed to flutter her lashes as she closed the door behind her.

Her smile faded, however, as she went into the kitchen and put some milk in a kettle to heat. As she spooned cocoa into mugs, she wondered just exactly how she should broach the news that Henry's studio apartment had been ransacked. There wasn't anything that the police could do, since the culprit had fled, and Cal definitely wasn't in any condition to tackle the problem until he had had a night's rest. The hot bath had obviously helped, but his face was still drawn with pain and fatigue.

At that moment he stuck his head around the door frame and said, "What happened to the robe that I had with me?"

Jessica closed her eyes for a moment and tried to visualize the living room upstairs. Certainly she hadn't left any robes lying around on the carpet. "Are you sure you had it in there?"

He frowned then, saying, "I thought so, but maybe not. I don't wear it much."

"Only for room service or in case of fire?"

"Something like that."

"Well, for now you'll have to hold court in bed or you'll walk around in your pajamas. This cocoa will be ready in a minute. I'll bring it in."

His mouth relaxed in a crooked grin. "Room service?"

Her own lips twitched, although she kept her voice stern. "Doctor's orders. And if you keep on arguing about it, I'll forget to put the cocoa in this hot milk."

That threat made him disappear in a hurry, and a moment later there was a creak of the springs as she heard him get into bed. She turned the stove burner to Warm under the kettle before she went into the bathroom to rescue his damp shirt and trousers from the floor. Fortunately they were both washable and it took only a moment to pile them on the small washing machine in the utility annex.

After that, she went back into the bath for a final tidying. She had to give him full marks for his housekeeping ventures; the mat was folded neatly, and only his wallet plus some loose change and keys were left on the counter by the basin to show he'd been there.

"You'll probably want to keep these closer," Jessica said, going into the bedroom with them. "What would you prefer—bureau or night table?"

Cal was propped up against the headboard and he grimaced as he saw what she was carrying. "Lord, I am getting careless." He gestured toward the night table. "This'll be fine, thanks."

A furtive smile played over her features. "It's all right," she assured him as she put them down. "I didn't check your wallet for identification cards, and I'll present a bill in the morning for your lodging, so you can relax on that score. You'll find thirty-seven cents in change without any deductions."

"I wasn't worried about that." His tone was dry but his half-closed eyes gleamed with laughter. "You're definitely the folding-money type."

Jessica wasn't sure whether that was a compliment.

"You can't count on that. I'll be back in a minute with a hot drink if you're okay."

"I'm perfectly fine," he said, trying to sound like it.

"You're also lying in your teeth, but I'll let you get away with it this time," she said over her shoulder as she headed back toward the kitchen.

When she returned a few minutes later carrying a streaming mug in either hand, she found him still leaning against the headboard with his eyes closed. As she hesitated on the threshold, his eyelids rose slowly and he bestowed a mocking glance. "If you stand there much longer you'll qualify as part of the furniture."

"And get painted the next time they redecorate," she acknowledged. "I was trying to decide whether or not to disturb your beauty sleep."

"Something tells me that I need it."

"Let's just say that I've seen people look better at the end of fifteen rounds." She handed over the mug. "Try some hot cocoa."

"At least it's a step up from hot milk," he said, taking a reluctant swallow.

"It's darned good and you know it." She perched on the end of the bed, carefully avoiding his long length stretched out under the covers. "This would be a good time to take those pills the doctor ordered."

"I suppose so." He frowned at the thought. "I'm sorry about all this."

"You really can't be blamed for getting a bump on the head. I'm just glad that you weren't stuck on the beach overnight. It's darned cold outside—even inside. That apartment of Henry's felt like an icebox . . ." Her voice trailed off as she debated telling him about the break-in, but a quick glance at his tired face made her decide that he was in no shape to cope with the problem until he'd had some rest. "Come on—take that last swallow with the pills."

"Bossy, too," Cal commented a moment later as he handed the empty mug to her.

"One of my more reprehensible traits. You can reflect on the rest of them after I turn out the light."

"I'll do that instead of counting sheep," he said with a crooked smile, sliding down into the bed when she paused by the door with her hand on the light switch. "Lord, this mattress feels good. Did I remember to thank you?"

"Don't worry about it. It'll all be included in the service charge on your bill. If you should want anything in the night . . ."

"Mmm?"

"I'll be nearby," she assured him, lingering a moment longer. "Just thump on the wall. Okay?"

"Uh-huh."

His response that time was barely discernible because he'd pulled the cocoon of covers around his head and clearly didn't want to prolong the conversation.

A slight smile came over her face and she backed out into the hall, leaving the bedroom door ajar so that she could hear if he did need help.

The ghostly sound of the foghorn atop the ferry landing area was punctuating the still air outside. Jessica went into the living room and stared through the big window onto the scene. Wisps of fog had settled over the boats anchored in front of the condominium like undersize blankets, hiked up just enough to reveal the dark water lapping around the hulls. For the first time the outlook gave her a feeling of claustrophobia, as if the enveloping gray mist contained all the horrors of the day. Cal's accident and even the break-in upstairs were part of that frightening package. Jessica found herself wishing for a sudden stiff wind to clear it away.

She tiptoed back down the hall, hesitating for a moment outside Cal's door. There was a faint rustling in the room as he tossed on the mattress, trying to get comfortable.

Every feminine instinct urged her to go in and ask him if there were anything she could do to help. Only the realization that he'd probably ask her exactly what she had in mind kept her away.

What she had in mind certainly wasn't part of the doctor's prescription. Jessica put her palms up to cool her suddenly hot cheeks. She thought distractedly that things had come to a pretty pass when her nerve ends started short-circuiting just because a presentable man was within reach.

The hot cocoa hadn't helped, and she wasn't enough of a masochist to contemplate a cold shower, so she marched in her bedroom to don her most tailored pair of pajamas. The fact that a slinky satin thigh-length robe completed the ensemble, and would come in handy if she had to look in on her patient in the middle of the night, had nothing to do with her decision.

She padded down the hall again when she'd brushed her teeth and washed her face. A check of the front-door lock was done carefully, and she made sure the security chain was in place as well. That time, she didn't hesitate as she made her way back to her bedroom and left her door wide open so that she could hear if he called.

For the next half-hour she tried to focus on a paperback novel, but after reading two chapters, she realized that she didn't have the faintest idea of the plot. She tossed it on the night table and reached across to turn off the light—sure that she wouldn't fall asleep after the day's excitement, but feeling she should make the effort.

It came as a great surprise, therefore, that the next sound to penetrate her consciousness was the whistle of the teakettle nearby. Before she could do more than push up on an elbow, the whistle was cut off abruptly. Jessica frowned, wondering if she'd dreamed it, and then her lips parted in amazement as she saw pale sunlight edging the window blinds.

The sudden silence made all the previous evening's happenings come flooding back. Evidently her patient had improved enough to decide against room service, or he was so desperate that he'd crawled out on his hands and knees to find a cup of instant coffee.

Jessica smiled as that image flashed in front of her, and she swung her feet out of bed, trying to find her slippers even as she reached for her robe atop the coverlet.

She was halfway to the doorway before detouring back to a mirror and her comb. After all, there was no point in completely disillusioning the man. Finally she smoothed the arch of her eyebrows and considered a light application of lipstick. It'd be a dead giveway, she decided, giving her reflection a frowning appraisal and putting her comb back on the counter.

She started toward the hallway at a brisk pace and then pulled up. A leisurely stroll was the way to go, and perhaps the slightest lifting of her eyebrows in surprise when she discovered him in the kitchen.

It was a blow to discover he wasn't in the kitchen after all. The sound of running water behind the

closed bathroom door showed that he'd changed his
locale while she'd been trying for the right ensemble.

"Damn!" she muttered, giving the door a lethal
glance. She stomped back to the kitchen and discovered an empty teakettle. It took only an instant to
refill it and put it on the burner, even as she debated
orange juice versus tomato juice. She was checking
the milk supply in the refrigerator when a sudden
thumping from the front porch brought her upright.
Another thump made her close the refrigerator, turn
off the stove, and head toward the porch. While she
had been understandably nervous in the ransacked
apartment upstairs the night before, she certainly
wasn't going to hesitate investigating in broad daylight.

Such determination didn't prevent her uttering a
startled shriek when a small body whipped past her
ankles as soon as she turned the knob and pulled the
door open.

She was still standing dazedly on the threshold,
watching a cat disappear into the shrubbery, when
the bathroom door was flung open and Cal emerged
to ask, "What's going on?"

Jessica turned a troubled face to him, admitting, "I
. . . I don't know. Something's in the kitchen."

He relaxed visibly. "No kidding. With Dinah, I
suppose."

"Don't be ridiculous! I mean it!"

He tightened his grip on the towel around his
waist, which was his only covering. "At least close
the door. It's drafty enough in here without heating
the whole waterfront."

"There are more important things than comfort
right now . . ." she began, and then hastily closed
the door behind her when she saw his jaw firm.
"Never mind the temperature," she went on before

he could retreat into the bathroom again. "Just go into the kitchen, will you? Something small and four-footed came calling a minute ago, and I didn't send out an invitation." As he started toward the kitchen archway, she put a hand on his arm to detain him. "You can't go like that—you haven't any shoes on."

"I didn't know it was formal," he retorted with some exasperation. "Do you want me to check this out or not?"

"Well, yes." She let her hand drop to her side, her fingers tingling from contact with the hard strength of his forearm. "But shouldn't you be carrying something?"

He shot her a look of amused resignation. "Exactly what did you have in mind? I only have two hands, and right now they're both keeping this towel in place. Of course, I could just trust to luck—"

"Never mind," she cut in hastily as she saw his fingers shift on the edge of it. "Whatever it was sort of slithered over my foot, so it can't be terribly dangerous."

His eyebrows went up. "Slithered?"

She chewed on the edge of her lip, trying to remember. "Sort of. Or maybe hopped. I think a cat was after it."

He shook his head, as if trying to clear it, and winced afterward. "Never mind. It doesn't sound lethal and it's certainly quiet in there," he added, starting toward the kitchen after securing his towel more firmly.

Jessica was on his heels as they crossed the threshold, and found herself more aware of the expanse of bare masculine shoulder in front of her than anything else. She drew an exasperated breath and tried to concentrate as she peered around him into the kitchen. The empty kitchen.

"Don't say it," she warned as he turned to face her with raised eyebrows an instant later. "I'm not imagining things. After all, you were the one hit on the head last night."

"I haven't forgotten," he said ruefully as he brought up a hand to rub the back of his neck. "But I still don't see hide nor hair of your uninvited caller. Are you sure—"

"Of course I'm sure," she interrupted, her tone higher than usual. "Maybe it's behind the refrigerator or something."

"No doubt. But as I'm scarcely dressed for the hunt," he said, tightening his towel, "maybe we can schedule it later. I don't think you'll have to worry about being attacked—at least above the ankles—while you're getting breakfast."

"Thanks very much," she said dryly. "That's a great comfort."

"Then I'll get dressed," he said, starting for the hall.

"Hadn't you better go back to bed and take it easy? You still don't look great."

"This is the way I always look in the morning," he informed her austerely, and closed the bedroom door behind him.

Jessica's mouth curved in a reluctant grin as she considered his last remark and acknowledged that perhaps her comment hadn't been very diplomatic. As she caught a glimpse of her reflection in a mirrored whatnot on the kitchen wall, she grimaced in disbelief. Talk about people in glass houses throwing stones! She looked like the wrath of heaven herself, but Cal, at least, hadn't commented on the fact.

An olive branch wouldn't be amiss, she told herself, and moved over to the stove to turn the burner on again under the teakettle. She walked gingerly, happy that her unknown intruder was staying out of sight for the moment.

As she started back toward her bedroom, she stopped at the open door of the utility room. Cal's muddied trousers and shirt were still where she'd put them last night. Washing his clothes would be a nice gesture, she told herself, and tossed them into the machine before setting the controls.

Water started pouring in while she was searching for detergent in a cupboard over the dryer. The opening of Cal's bedroom door must have been drowned out by the filling washer, because the first inkling she had of his presence on the scene was when his bare arm shot over her shoulder to open the washer and cut off the water supply.

"I hope to God you didn't . . . Oh, hell!" He was delving frantically into the machine as he spoke, pulling out his dripping trousers.

Jessica's eyes grew wide. "What's the matter? They *are* washable, aren't they? They certainly didn't look as if they had to be dry-cleaned." Her voice trailed off as she saw him extract a plastic wallet from the back pocket. "Oh, no!" she moaned. "They're not—"

"Traveler's checks," he confirmed with a tight jaw. "Definitely not washable. I was just lucky my pocket stayed dry last night."

"I'm sorry. I had no idea."

Her woebegone expression must have gotten through to him, because his tone was considerably more friendly as he dropped the trousers back into the water and started leafing through the checks. "It's okay—the top one's sort of waterlogged, but the rest can be salvaged. They'll just be crinkled around the edges."

"Thank heaven." She exhaled audibly and rubbed her forehead with the back of her hand. "I get the feeling that this is going to be one of those days."

"I know what you mean. Yesterday wasn't a great one for me." He glanced toward the kitchen as the kettle started whistling. "Maybe coffee will improve things."

"There's only one way to go," she agreed, starting toward the stove. "Are you interested in a cup?"

"Give me five minutes."

"Take your time. I'm still in shock after nearly sending your bank account down the drain. Imagine having to explain that to a stony-faced banker."

His lips twitched. "I'm sure you would have done it beautifully."

"I'm not so sure," she said shaking her head. "Things haven't been going very well ever since I appeared on the scene yesterday."

Her casual comment seemed to have a more profound effect on him than she'd anticipated. Even as she watched, his glance narrowed and became appraising. His next words made her wonder if their relationship had even progressed beyond square one. "I was thinking about that myself," he said in a considering tone.

"Well, I didn't hit you over the head and then come back in a half-hour to rescue you because I'd had a change of heart—no matter how it seems. And if I'd planned any other horrors"—she ignored his muttered comment to press home her point—"you'd never have made it through the night."

"That wasn't what I meant," he managed to say.

"I'm glad, because I could still put arsenic in your coffee, or whatever's available."

"I'd better give you a chance to root through the kitchen and find out," he said dryly, starting toward the bedroom again. "I'll be in better condition to meet my fate with some clothes on." He had taken only a couple of steps before he stopped and made a production of retrieving the damp packet of traveler's checks from the counter before disappearing into the bedroom.

Jessica watched, stony-eyed, as the door slammed behind him. It was a pity that she didn't have a supply of ground glass on hand to do something drastic, because at that particular moment she would have been tempted to use it.

4

Jessica had just taken a swallow of coffee and was still standing in the middle of the kitchen when a determined knocking came on the front door.

She said "Damn!" in a fervent undertone before realizing that the first intruder of the morning hadn't bothered to knock. That meant she was certainly capable of handling this one. A renewed tattoo made her hasten to the door, still holding her coffee because she had forgotten to put it down.

"Oh, it's you," she said, seeing Valerie Long as she pulled it open. Then, realizing that she scarcely sounded welcoming, she managed to put some enthusiasm in her voice. "I mean—good morning. You sort of surprised me. Won't you come in?"

The secretary managed a semblance of a smile, but she didn't take advantage of the wider door, staying resolutely on the threshold as she said, "No, that isn't necessary. I know it's too early to come calling, but I wondered if you knew where Cal is. We had a date for breakfast but there doesn't seem to be any answer up at his apartment." She managed a bright smile that didn't reach her eyes as she added, "I realized that it's an outside chance, but—" her voice gurgled to a stop as they heard footsteps in the hall.

"Hello, Val." Cal sounded completely unruffled as he appeared beside Jessica. "Sorry to keep you waiting for our date. I'm running a little behind schedule this morning."

"So I notice." Valerie didn't attempt to cloak her disdain as she took in his unbuttoned sport shirt, casual slacks, and bare feet. "You're a little informal—even for the island." Her glance went to Jessica, letting it linger on her pajamas and thigh-length robe. "Quite informal."

Jessica felt her cheeks redden as she thought how they had changed roles. Valerie had abandoned her "earth-mother" costume of the day before and looked sleekly attractive in a dress with a crisp white top and slim gray skirt which showed her waistline to the best possible advantage. Her flat shoes had been discarded in favor of high-heeled black pumps which weren't in the least practical but did wonders for flattering the secretary's long legs.

Jessica's glance slid on to Cal, catching him in the middle of an appreciative survey of his own. "You look even more gorgeous than usual," he said to Valerie with a smile. "I'd better go upstairs and put on something more presentable if I'm taking you out."

"Then you haven't moved in here to stay?" Valerie's tone was arch.

Jessica got tired of being ignored and cut in before he had a chance to reply. "Hardly. The heat isn't turned on upstairs so I was doing the good-neighbor bit." She paused to see if Cal would interrupt to mention his mishap, but he merely waited for her to go on with her explanation. She continued, trying to sound as if male guests who spent the night were commonplace in her life. "The temperature was certainly more comfortable down here. At least there was heat."

"I can imagine." Valerie kept her voice sweet. "And all the conveniences too."

"Which I took advantage of," Cal said blandly, ignoring her double meaning. "Including a twenty-four-hour laundry service that I certainly hadn't expected."

"It was no trouble at all," Jessica said, smiling back at him with an effort. Definitely, she should have stocked up on ground glass!

"I hate to break this up," Valerie said, "but if I'm to get to work on time, we'd better be on our way." She glanced at Cal. "Did you mean it about going upstairs to change?"

He gestured at his rumpled clothes. "I certainly did. They'd pull me in for vagrancy if I appeared at breakfast like this."

"Hardly that drastic." She patted his arm. "I don't mind waiting a few more minutes with you upstairs while you change."

"Upstairs!" Jessica gasped at Valerie's comment suddenly penetrated. Her head turned toward Cal as she said, "You can't . . . I mean . . . it isn't necessary."

"What isn't?" He was obviously perplexed but his voice was unconcerned. "If you'd like to join us for breakfast, you'd be more than welcome. Isn't that right, Val?"

There was a perceptible pause while the secretary struggled to say the right thing. "I wouldn't dream of it," Jessica put in hurriedly, "thanks all the same." She fixed Cal with an imploring look as she went on, "There's something I have to tell you."

Valerie's lips thinned. "Surely it could wait until another time."

"It'll only take a moment," Jessica assured her, and tugged Cal toward the hallway. "If you'll excuse us, please . . ."

"What in the devil's going on?" he demanded as he let himself be pulled to the master bedroom.

"I'm sorry. I should have explained earlier."

"Can't it wait?" He turned to face her as she closed the bedroom door behind them. "I'll be back in a couple hours at the most."

She shook her head. "It isn't that. I really should have told you last night. It's your apartment upstairs. Or Henry's. Or whoever's. Anyhow, somebody broke in and went through your things." As she watched his expression darken, she went on doggedly, "Nothing seemed to have been taken—at least the television and stereo were still there."

He waved that aside. "Why in the hell didn't you mention it last night?"

"Because you didn't look as if you were in any condition for the news. And because whoever did it was long gone. I just thought you should know before you took Valerie up there this morning."

"Why?" He shot her a frowning look. "Surely you don't think she had anything to do with it."

"No, of course not. It's just that . . . well, things are a little scattered around. I didn't want you both to walk in cold."

" 'Cold' is certainly the operative word," he said, rubbing a bare foot against his trouser leg. "I don't seem to have recovered from lying around out there yet. That beach was damn cold!" He let out a sigh and shook his head. "I guess I'd better send Valerie along to the restaurant and catch her up later."

"She won't like it."

His grin was rueful as he reached for the door-knob. "Why don't you tell me something I don't know. You might stay out of sight until she's on her way. Let me have your car keys, will you? I'll have my pal at the service station go out and retrieve your car."

"Won't he think it's strange?"

"Not if I say you'd been having engine trouble and hitched a ride home."

"All right." She fished in her purse and pulled out a duplicate set to give to him. "Just have him park it in the garage and lock the keys in the glove compartment. I guess I won't need it this morning." Jessica sank onto the side of the bed. "Will I see you later?" It was an effort to keep her tone uncaring, but she managed.

"Oh, yes. We still have some things to discuss. I should be back in an hour and a half," he said before closing the door after him.

Evidently he was taking no chances of another confrontation between her and Valerie, Jessica thought. She watched the dial of her bedside clock and heard the outer door of the apartment close two minutes later. After that, she waited another three minutes to make sure the coast was clear before padding back to the kitchen to eat breakfast in solitary grandeur.

Once she'd finished her cereal and was on a second cup of coffee, she walked out in the living room to stare at the water. At any other time she would have been fascinated by the scene in front of her—the stern of a huge Washington State ferry disappearing around the shore of the island on its way back to the mainland and a brightly-colored float plane taxiing down the quieter waters of the cove. In front of the apartment the crew of that imposing sailboat was shifting supplies, obviously getting ready to cruise the San Juans. Jessica stood watching quietly, but her thoughts were anything but quiet—almost as chaotic as the antics of the German shepherd that was supervising the loading with happy staccato barks. Jessica smiled ruefully, realizing that she wasn't making any more headway than the dog was. Probably the logical thing would have been to go straight to the police after she'd taken Cal to the doctor the night before. Certainly she should have called them after discovering the break-in at the apartment. Instead, she was waiting around, meekly following orders from a man who liked giving them.

She turned to pick up the phone and then shook her head, perching hesitantly on the end of the davenport instead.

She could always call Henry in the hospital and add to his misery by telling him that his apartment had been broken into overnight. "That would really be brilliant," she muttered in an undertone. "With luck, I could give him a relapse."

She took another swallow of coffee and then got up to walk down the hallway to her bedroom. Probably she owed it to Cal to at least listen to his explanation, and then she'd make a decision as to what she wanted to do. After all, she reasoned, it wasn't as if she were in danger. The only thing that had concentrated on her in the last twelve hours had slithered over her instep and was remaining out of sight.

"And I hope to God it stays that way," she murmured, shedding her robe and pajamas to go in the shower.

Afterward, it didn't take her long to don a pale green silk shirt and matching linen skirt. A glance in the mirror when she'd finished applying a very special shade of lipstick made her nod with satisfaction. Valerie would find that she didn't have things all her way in the fashion competition. The soft green was a decided success with dark red hair. Not that it mattered, she told herself as she put the cap back on the lipstick and tossed it in her purse. After all, who was there to impress other than the real-estate man she planned to visit later that morning?

She moved quickly away from the mirror at that blatant prevarication and went back in the living room, picking up a white blazer on the way. Damned if she'd hang around waiting for Cal's arrival!

She relented to the point of leaving a brief note on the counter saying that she'd return within the hour, and went out into the sunshine.

She was so engrossed in her thoughts that she almost collided with a man on the path in front of the apartments. "I'm sorry," she began, sidestepping to get out of his way. "I should have been looking where I was going."

"My fault, I'm afraid," he said, shifting the box of provisions he was carrying. "Hey, wait a minute, didn't I see you yesterday? When I was with Cal Sloane? I'm Bruce Lightner—from the real-estate office on Main Street."

"Of course." Her gesture was apologetic. "You look different today."

"The jeans, you mean?" His grin made his middle-aged features suddenly more youthful. "Today I'm all set to play. Can I tempt you with a sail?"

"I don't think I'd better." Jessica decided it wasn't a good time to tell him that she'd planned to send some business his way if he'd stayed in his office.

"Do you belong to that boat with the dog? I mean, does that dog belong to you?"

He laughed at her attempt to put it in a more flattering light. "Actually you've hit the nail on the head. Kai thinks he owns the whole shebang."

"Kai?"

"For the Kaiser." He shifted the box of provisions to get a better hold on it. "Most of this stuff is dog food."

"Then I'd better let you get on your way or he'll come up here to find out what's wrong. I'd hate to be on the wrong side of him."

"He knows who his friends are." Bruce gave her a friendly nod. "Next time, I'll let you have more notice on my invitation. You'll be staying on the island for a bit, won't you?"

"A while," she replied noncommittally.

The answer seemed to satisfy him. "Fine. I'll be going, then." He started down the path again and then stopped abruptly to ask. "Have you seen Cal this morning, by any chance?"

Jessica opened her mouth to say that he was uptown sharing a table for breakfast and then thought better of it. "Your friend? Is he among the missing?" She waved in an airy gesture: "I'm not surprised—it must be hard to get any work done in this beautiful weather."

Bruce nodded agreeably. "Knowing Cal, he's probably goofing off. If you happen to see him around, you might mention that I was asking."

"I'll do that." Jessica turned and started determinedly down the path toward the shops, wanting to get out of the vicinity before she ran into Cal on his return. Kai started barking again and then stopped abruptly after a sharp command. Apparently Bruce

Lightner had decided that some discipline was necessary aboard.

It was kind of him to invite her for a sail, she thought as she walked along the narrow path. Any other time, she would have taken him up on it because his big sailboat was certainly outfitted with every accessory, from the radar reflector mounted below the spreaders to the shining brass binnacle. She doubted if he had any trouble finding guests for a cruise with such luxurious accommodations. At least it was satisfying to her ego that *somebody* wanted her around after her morning's encounter with Cal and Valerie.

She was almost at the gate separating the condominium complex from shops on the public pier when Cal suddenly appeared around the corner. He pulled up abruptly on seeing her and snapped, "I thought I told you to wait for me at the apartment."

Jessica took a deep breath and managed to keep her voice level. "Did you really? It must have slipped my mind." She reached out to hold the gate ajar so she could slip through it. "I'm sorry to rush, but there are some errands I have to run—what do you think you're doing?" The last words came in an angry crescendo as he spun her around, frog-marching her back down the path she'd just traveled.

"I know what *I'm* doing," he retorted. "What's your excuse?"

"I don't need any," she flared back, managing to pull to a stop. "And I'm damned well not taking orders from you."

"You'd rather break your word—is that it? You promised—"

"I did *not* promise," she broke in, trying desperately to remember if she had actually told him she'd wait.

"That isn't the way I remember the conversation. Anyhow, there wasn't any doubt in my mind." His angry tone softened as he went on. "I could use some help."

"I thought Valerie was taking care of that category."

"Then you got it all wrong. We merely shared a couple of croissants—not our life stories."

"Well . . ."

He took her wavering tone as acceptance and gave her a gentle nudge back on the path. "Good. Did you catch another glimpse of our four-footed intruder?" he asked conversationally as they strolled along.

She shook her head. "All quiet in the living room, and there weren't any beady eyes staring around the teakettle, so I guess I can relax. As a matter of fact, I had the territory completely to myself except for catching a glimpse of a German shepherd and running into Bruce Lightner a few minutes ago. Well, not actually running into him, but almost . . ." Her words trailed off as Cal stopped walking. "Now what?"

He ignored that. "What was Bruce doing?"

"Going for a sail. He invited me along, but I turned him down." Her eyes widened as Cal caught her elbow and spun her around again. "I wish you'd stop that," she complained. "I'm getting dizzy."

"Sorry." He didn't sound particularly remorseful and he kept a firm grip on her elbow as they went down the path. "You reminded me of something."

"I'm glad you have an excuse." She looked up at the windows of the condominiums they were passing. "If anybody's watching, they'll think we're losing our collective minds."

"Maybe it'll give them a cheap thrill—there's not much front-page news in this place, or news of any kind." He didn't slacken his pace as he asked,

"How do you feel about going for a boat ride with me?"

Jessica almost tripped as she stared up at him. "What kind of boat?"

"The usual." He sounded amused. "Why? Are you particular?"

"They come in different sizes," she pointed out, aware that he was still clutching her elbow as if afraid she'd bolt down the path. "Starting with ferries and working your way down."

"This is considerably smaller. And smaller than Bruce's, too—if you had that one in mind."

"Bigger than a bread box but smaller than a rowboat." She turned to face him as they reached the gate again. "If we're playing Twenty Questions, this could take a while."

"Relax—it's a twenty-five-foot sailboat with a better-than-average motor, so you don't have to worry about getting home again."

"I wasn't worried. Where is it?"

"Down at the public marina." He gestured in that direction. "How long will it take you to get ready?"

She blinked and glanced down at her outfit. "I guess I'm ready now. If I remembered my sunglasses . . ." She patted her purse and nodded.

"You might need a sweater out on the water, but you can borrow one of mine. I usually leave some gear aboard."

"Hold on a minute." She managed to extricate her elbow when he would have steered her through the gate. "You mean this is your boat."

"In a manner of speaking." He went through the gate himself, apparently sure that she'd follow. "We'll have to pick up something for lunch."

"That may be important to your way of thinking,

but you've ignored a few things at the top of my list. I don't know whether you're related to Jack the Ripper or even why you're in the neighborhood. And there's the little matter of getting hit over the head and having your apartment ransacked." She fixed him with an accusing look. "Plus a brunette who comes calling very early in the morning!"

"It's good to know we agree on the main topics," he said, setting a businesslike pace as they walked along the small shops edging the ferry pier.

"What do you mean?"

"Just that we should put the brunette, my ancestry, and injuries on hold for the moment." He paused in front of a deli window. "Does pastrami sound good to you?"

She threw up her hands in disgust. "I give up."

"It's easier that way. The pastrami's especially good on the dark rye here. Add a couple of ham and cheese too." He glanced at his watch before reaching in his wallet to pull out some currency. "We might have to stretch it to two meals, so pick up anything that looks good."

"Wait a minute! Where are you going?"

"Just up to that phone booth at the end of the pier," he said, gesturing as he spoke. "I have to cancel an appointment."

"I see," Jessica murmured, only halfway amused to find that she was addressing the middle of his back as he strode off again. She hesitated a moment, wondering if that appointment was a lunch date with the same brunette, or even another one. The latter suspicion came as she noticed Cal greeting an attractive slender woman who was unlocking a craft shop near the phone booth he'd mentioned. It was clear that he hadn't been avoiding the social scene since he'd been on the island.

Jessica sniffed in annoyance and pulled open the door of the delicatessen with more force than necessary.

Cal was right about the quality of food on display and she found herself planning a picnic lunch with more enthusiasm than she would have believed. Ten minutes later she emerged carrying a bulging bag of groceries.

Cal grinned as he came down the boardwalk to relieve her of the parcel. "All set?"

"I guess so." She nodded toward the empty phone booth. "How about you? Any complications?"

His eyes narrowed. "Not really. Why? Did you think there might be?"

She heaved an exasperated sigh. "Every time I ask a question, I find myself answering one of yours."

"Is that a fact?" His eyebrows climbed at her stormy expression and he made an attempt to placate her. "Sorry. It's still a little early for serious conversation. You'll feel better once we're on the water."

"I feel fine right now," she flared in response, and then lowered her tone under his reproving look. "Maybe it is a little early," she admitted, suddenly aware that she wouldn't get anywhere losing her temper. In fact, she might possibly be left on the dock while Cal sailed off into the horizon.

"Thatta girl," he said idly. Jessica decided that he wasn't really listening to the conversation, and her suspicion was confirmed when he set off briskly down the walk leading to the marina without any more discussion.

She had to dogtrot to keep up with his long steps, but she managed. She was relieved a few minutes later when he had to slow his progress as they reached the broad wooden walkway leading down to the piers. Even though it was still early, there was considerable activity in the marina; the ice booth was doing a thriving business, as was the bait cubicle alongside, where boaters lined up to spend money. There was a buzz of conversation as the power boat and sailboat skippers perched on the rails nearby, coffee mugs in hand, and discussed the local news.

The snippets Jessica overheard mostly concerned their social activities of the night before, and her cheeks were definitely warmer by the time Cal turned off and led her down a small side pier.

"There she is," he said a moment or two later as he pulled up by the bow of a small sailboat. Then, as he turned to see her reaction, he frowned. "What's the matter? You look done in."

She put up her palms to cool her cheeks, saying, "There's nothing the matter with me. I'm just not used to walking so fast." She waved a hand at the sailboat, which was neat but not impressive. "It doesn't look very big."

"Fortunately the motor is," Cal said, going nimbly down the finger pier alongside the boat and stepping over the rail without any hesitation. "We may put up the sails later, but right now I'm feeling lazy." He deposited the bag containing their picnic lunch and then turned to see Jessica still standing by the bow. "Come aboard. You don't need a formal invitation on a twenty-five-footer."

Jessica looked at the foot-wide slip and the dark water below it. Her sense of balance wasn't great and the noise of the currents lapping against the hull didn't help her confidence.

"What are you waiting for?" Cal asked, clearly puzzled by her indecision.

For an instant she was tempted to brazen it out, and then the motion of the boat at the next pier got to her. "I'm sorry," she said grimly, "but the only way I'd be sure of making it would be on my hands and knees."

"Sorry." His response was quick in coming and he was back on the pier, offering to give her a hand almost before she finished speaking. "Here—hang on to me." His stern mouth softened in a rueful grin. "It's the least I can do after last night."

"Yes, but you had an excuse," she told him, grateful for his steady grip as she stepped onto the boat. "I'd never make it on a balance beam." She sat down by the side of the tiller and tucked her feet under her so that she wouldn't get in his way.

"That's all right—you don't have to work your passage on a boat this size." He was releasing the bowline as he spoke, and came swiftly back to settle at the stern. In no time at all he'd coaxed a muted roar from the motor and thrust the tiller extension into Jessica's hands. "Hang on to this until I get us free."

She clutched the tiller for the few seconds it took him to cast off the stern line and then sat back as he took over again. The small boat was maneuvered out of the slip without a wasted motion, and the pitch of the motor rose as he increased the power when they headed toward the channel.

As soon as they hit the open water, the sailboat rose and fell in a gentle rhythm and Jessica decided to relax. She put on her dark glasses and slid along the bench to rest comfortably against the cabin bulkhead, which let her enjoy the sunshine and find shelter from the breeze. It was merely coincidence that her perch gave her an unobstructed view of Cal's relaxed figure at the tiller.

In view of what had happened to him in the last twenty-four hours, he should have been close to a basket case, she thought, half-closing her eyes as she surveyed him. He still looked as if he were feeling the effects of that bump on the head but she knew better than to comment on it. The perfect example of a stoic American male with a "never explain, never complain" philosophy. Her lips twitched, remembering how her brother subscribed to the same idea.

"Something funny?" Cal's drawled question showed that he wasn't unaware of her appraisal.

"Family joke," she evaded, and then sat up straighter to say, "I think this is an excellent time to lay some of your cards on the table. Like why you were hit over the head and why people are rooting around in that apartment you and Henry are sharing."

Cal sighed and adjusted the motor before answering. "If I knew the answers to those two, I'd be happier myself."

Jessica shoved her sunglasses down on her nose to glare over them. "Now, look here, you're not going to get away with evasive answers this time. I don't even know what you're doing here on the island. The first day we met, I saw you disappearing into the crew's quarters on the ferry, and I thought you belonged there, but Henry scotched that idea."

"Ah, yes—Henry. I'm surprised that he hasn't given you all the answers you want."

She shoved the glasses slowly back into place as she shook her head. "I didn't want to bother him at first. Even now, it hardly seems fair to badger him."

"But he *did* set you straight on the nonexistent ferry connection."

"He just said that you had a friend who was an officer on one of them." Jessica brushed her hair back from her face as he altered their course and a gust of wind swept over the stern. "As a matter of fact, Henry seems to think that you're on some kind of an extended holiday, which you can well afford. His words, not mine," she added when Cal's eyebrows came together.

There was a perceptible pause before he said, "I may have convinced him, but I have my doubts about you. Am I right?"

"All the way. If you were taking a vacation, it wouldn't be in this backwater."

"More the Cote d'Azur type?" He sounded amused. "Or Cannes in season?"

She pursed her lips, considering. "No. You don't strike me as the kind who'd seek out topless beaches. Maybe the Canaries or Scotland for golf."

"You've obviously never seen me on a putting green." He shook his head. "Sorry, but you won't make it reading tea leaves. How do you earn a living?"

Jessica opened her mouth to tell him and then closed it again. There was an instant's pause while she made a production out of looking over the rail before saying, "I almost followed that red herring. Nice try, Mr. Sloane, but I asked first."

His lips tightened momentarily, but that was the only sign of his annoyance, and a second later he gave a reluctant chuckle. "Okay. Believe it or not, this started out as a vacation. Then I ran into some friends of mine who said they could use some help. Unfortunately the San Juans have turned into a major pipeline for contraband—there's a lot of room up here, and surveillance by the authorities is difficult."

Jessica's eyes grew wider as he spoke. "Good Lord! I had no idea. Of course, I've read about the drug problem. The stuff starts out in the Far East, doesn't it?"

There was a perceptible pause while Cal was obviously weighing his words, and then he said, "That's one of the major sources."

"And of course, I've read about the Colombian connection too," Jessica said, delighted that she could discuss the problem intelligently. "Although Florida is the main target for East Coast distribution." She frowned then before saying hesitantly, "I still don't understand what that has to do with Henry and the fire. Surely you don't suspect him? Most of the time he doesn't even know what century he's in."

"I didn't say I did," Cal said patiently. "And arson doesn't necessarily go hand in hand with every problem."

Jessica absently moved her arm back from the rail when another gust of wind brought a shower of salt spray into the boat. "It's a good thing it's warm," she said, brushing droplets of water from her blouse. "Maybe I should have packed a swimsuit."

"There's a rain jacket down in the cabin."

She surveyed the front of her shirt and then shook her head. "No need—unless the wind freshens or we change course. You didn't say where we're going."

"You didn't give me a chance. I thought we'd hug the shore for a mile or so and keep an eye out for the Orca pod that's been hanging around."

Jessica interrupted excitedly. "You mean it?" Has there been a good sighting recently?"

"I heard a report at breakfast that there was a pod close to the Canadian boundary and they were supposed to be headed in this general direction. At least I can guarantee seals." He gestured toward a small rock islet ahead of them on the right. "It looks like a convention of them enjoying the sun."

"How wonderful!" she exclaimed, fascinated by the sight of so many sleek, lazy beasts basking in the warm breeze while draping themselves over the rocky contours of the small island. "Could we possibly get a little closer without spooking them?"

"I don't think there's a clenched paw in that whole bunch," Cal remarked, but he throttled down the motor and maneuvered to get closer. "Too bad we didn't bring a camera."

"I know. It doesn't really matter. I'm probably the world's worst photographer."

"No talent, eh?"

"Only at cutting off heads and putting my finger in front of the lens. I've been known to do both on the same picture." She gestured toward an especially well-fed seal on the nearest rock, who'd raised his head to survey them lazily. "He looks like the keeper of the harem."

"Could be." Cal shifted to ask her, "Had enough?"

"I think so." She settled back against the bulkhead as he headed out toward the channel again and increased speed. "What's next on the agenda?"

"We'll take a turn at whale-watching and then pull into a cove below Cattle Point for lunch if that sounds good."

"Perfect." Jessica narrowed her eyes thoughtfully, surveying his relaxed figure at the helm. "You're being awfully nice."

His shoulders shook. "It only happens on odd Tuesdays."

"I'll remember," she assured him solemnly, and then closed her eyes to bask contentedly in the sunshine as he kept the boat on a steady course around the island.

It took about a half-hour before they entered waters that the Orca pod had been frequenting during the past week. Jessica was pressed into service again at the tiller while Cal disappeared into the small cabin, emerging a moment or so later carrying two pairs of binoculars. He took charge of the tiller again after handing one pair to Jessica with instructions to "start looking."

She obediently scanned the surrounding waters, hoping to see the gleaming black-and-white bodies of the famed Orcas as they performed their exciting ballet-type movements.

Finally she lowered the binoculars and glanced across at Cal, who was sitting with one leg casually hooked over the tiller while using the other pair of glasses. "See anything?" she asked hopefully.

He shook his head. " 'Fraid not. Looks as if we've struck out for the time being. How about heading in and anchoring for lunch? We can try our luck at whale-watching afterward."

She nodded and wound the leather cord around the glasses before shoving them back in the case. "That's probably the best plan. We can still keep an eye on the channel while we're eating."

"Right." He put his glasses down beside him and revved the motor to head for the shoreline. "At least you'll have a chance to improve your tan."

"It looks as if we'll have plenty of company." She gestured behind them. "There's a steady stream of power boats back there. Even a couple of good-size sailboats."

Cal glanced over his shoulder and then brought the glasses up for a quick look where she'd indicated. He put them down again without comment and kept on a steady course toward the cove.

It took just a few minutes more before he found the spot he was seeking for an anchorage. Jessica stayed out of the way as he deftly switched off the motor and then made his way forward to drop anchor.

They were close enough to the overhanging cliff that she could hear the cheerful twittering of some small birds on the branches of a cedar that prevailing chinook winds had pushed into a grotesque configuration above them. Interspersed with the chorus was the occasional cry of a shorebird as it swooped downward.

Jessica glanced over her shoulder to stare out at the channel they'd just abandoned while Cal ducked into the cabin to get their lunch. It was a beautiful day, she mused as she noted the bright sunlight reflecting from the gunmetal-gray water. The strong-current areas could be traced with the riffles along the surface. In the center of one, a deadhead of timber was moving surprisingly fast, and Jessica's thoughts reverted to the memory of Cal's inert body lying half in the water the night before. Flotsam of a different type. She shuddered and deliberately turned her glance to the south, concentrating on rocky islets with tufts of grass growing on their tops. Far beyond them, Mount Baker's snow-capped summit provided a spectacular background, hovering over the scene like a benevolent elder statesman.

"Hey! What are you doing?"

Jessica's startled question was cut off as Cal slid onto the bench and pulled her on his lap in one deft motion. With his free hand he grasped the back of her neck and, an instant later, she found her face against his tanned throat.

It was an effort to push back from his iron grip, but she managed to get free enough to protest, "For Pete's sake—let go of me. I can't breathe!"

"Calm down," came his firm voice in her ear. "You're breathing." His clasp tightened as he shifted position, and he lowered his head to nuzzle the deep V of her blouse. Ruthlessly pushing aside her collar, he sought the soft skin underneath, and Jessica's pulse rate bounded like a wild thing. Then she moaned softly as his lips forged a trail around the curve of her breast and her last resistance disappeared under mounting delight.

It seemed years later when she whispered, "I don't know exactly what you have in mind, but this isn't the place."

"Just relax," he said, and held her even more firmly on his lap.

For the first time, she became aware of engine noise gradually fading as it came across the water, and she pulled free long enough to see the stern of a large sailboat disappearing from the cove. "Isn't that . . . ?" She paused, trying to sort out her chaotic thoughts.

"Bruce's boat," Cal supplied calmly. "You can get up now," he said, dropping his hands and sitting upright. "If you want to," he added dryly as she blinked in dazed fashion and remained where she was. "Personally I'm quite comfortable."

"Well, I'm not." Jessica lurched onto the bench she'd occupied earlier. "Maybe you'll tell me what that was all about."

"It just seemed like the simplest way of avoiding company." Cal sounded offhand as he reached into the bag containing their lunch. "What kind of sandwich do you want?"

"I don't *care* what kind . . ." Jessica took another deep breath to settle her pulse rate. "It doesn't matter. Why couldn't you just disappear in the cabin?"

"It wouldn't have been diplomatic." Cal tossed her a sandwich and selected another for himself before digging in the bag again for paper cups. "We have a real-estate deal cooking and I don't want to do anything to put the kibosh on it."

"What about my reputation?" Jessica tried not to sound bitter in the face of his casual attitude.

"I don't think he got a very good look at you. Of course, that outfit you're wearing does sort of stick out in a crowd."

Jessica's lips thinned as she remembered the price tag on her "outfit." When she'd bought it, she'd hoped for more than just sticking out in a crowd.

"Don't you like the sandwich?"

His question made her realize that she was still chewing her first bite. "It's okay. Why?"

"You looked as if you'd found something walking around in the lettuce."

"Not in the lettuce. No, thanks. Not right now." The last came as he offered her coffee. She tried for a casual tone as she went on, "Are you thinking of buying a permanent home here on the island?"

"I'm not sure. Why?"

"Believe it or not, I'm just making lunchtime conversation," she lied. "And I wish to heaven you'd stop asking *me* questions."

He gave her a thoughtful look before pulling a pair of dark glasses from his shirt pocket and putting them on. "You seem upset all of a sudden."

"That's absurd." She took another defiant bite of her sandwich, hoping he wouldn't discover that she was practically a wreck after an embrace that was only camouflage on his part. A surreptitious glance at him confirmed her suspicions; he was munching away on his sandwich with evident appetite, as if nothing had happened. Jessica managed to swallow a mouthful of bread and realized that she'd never make it through the first course. "Could I change my mind about the coffee?" she asked.

"Sure thing."

As he rummaged by his side for the thermos, she managed to slip half of her sandwich overboard and kept the remainder shrouded by a napkin as she reached for the cup he held out. "I was thirstier than I thought. It must be all this fresh air," she said, ignoring his quizzical glance.

"Umm. No doubt."

Another sideways glance made Jessica aware that perhaps she wasn't the only one who was playing two roles. While Cal's thoughts hadn't affected his appetite, his attention was patently divided between matters aboard and keeping a constant survey of the marine traffic beyond the cove.

"Anything interesting?" Jessica asked casually when he shifted to get a better view as the boat moved on the anchor chain.

He looked around, frowning. "What do you mean?"

"I thought you'd caught sight of that Orca pod."

"Oh, that." Cal must have realized he wasn't following the proper script and made an effort to sound disappointed. " 'Fraid we're out of luck with them," he said, surveying his wristwatch as if he were responsible for the countdown at Canaveral. "Too late in the day for an appearance now. We'd better give it a try another time. Okay with you?"

The last comment was an obvious afterthought. Jessica knew he expected her to murmur a noncom-

mittal acceptance but decided that he wasn't going to
have it quite so easy. "Do we have to?" she asked,
swallowing her coffee and handing the cup back for a
refill. "After all, what's the hurry? It's such a pretty
day, it really doesn't matter whether we catch up
with the whales or not." She stretched in a leisurely
way and settled again on her perch, resting her back
against the cabin bulkhead. "I could spend the rest of
the day here in the cove. You know, I just realized
why it seems so quiet—I haven't heard the hum of an
air conditioner since I left Texas."

"Up here, an air conditioner comes in the same
category as an icebox for Eskimos." Cal kept his tone
pleasant with obvious effort. "I really think we'd
better cut it short today."

"Must we?"

Her woebegone expression didn't work. "You'll
thank me later," he said dryly. "After tossing most of
your sandwich overboard, you'll be ready for an
early dinner. Hang on to the tiller for a minute,
while I raise the anchor."

Jessica found herself being moved to the stern before she had a chance to protest, and her angry look
slid off the back of his shoulders as he made his way
to the bow and the anchor line. A moment or two
later, he came swiftly back to the stern and set about
starting the motor. His look of concentration changed
to one of satisfaction once the engine erupted into a
muted roar, and he reached for the tiller again, giving
Jessica the barest nod of acknowledgment.

She decided not to go down to defeat without one
last try. "Can we take a scenic loop back? I'd like to
see how the southern end of the island has changed.
Apparently there's been a lot of development."

"So Bruce tells me. I thought it was just real-estate

hype but maybe you could confirm it for me. You'll have to take a drive down that way in the next day or so." Even as he spoke, he was pointing the bow toward the channel they'd traversed earlier—the direct way back to Friday Harbor.

He was completely matter-of-fact. Jessica had a mad moment, expecting that his next words would be "Take a letter, Miss Webster" or "Your expense account's late—get it in on time next month." She shook her head, dispelling such flights of fancy, but the basic premise didn't go away; that so-called sentimental interlude hadn't left the slightest imprint on Cal Sloane. Obviously the man had other things on his mind, no matter how he tried to disguise it. And since his change of mood had come about at the same time as Bruce Lightner and his sailboat—they seemed to be responsible.

"You're very quiet."

Cal's thoughtful comment brought her head up abruptly. "Am I?" she said, stalling for time. "It must be the effect of the sunshine and salt water." She scrunched in her corner and pushed her sunglasses up on her nose. "This seems like a good time for a nap. Try not to hit the dock too hard when we get back to the marina—I like to wake up slowly."

She had the satisfaction of seeing an annoyed expression on his chiseled features before she closed her eyes and retreated behind her own wall of silence.

5

The trip back to the marina was certainly peaceful. If Jessica hadn't been so annoyed by Cal's reticence, she probably would have fallen asleep under the somnambulistic combination of lapping waves, salt spray, and gentle sunlight.

She did manage to keep her eyes closed for most of the journey. However, when she stretched and pretended to awaken as Cal cut the motor alongside the dock, she noticed that his expression was skeptical as she met his gaze.

"Can I help with anything?" she asked, ignoring his mood.

"No, thanks," he said, getting to his feet and moving swiftly forward. "The way things are going, you'd probably fall overboard."

His comment came as he put over some fenders so they wouldn't scrape the dock before he made fast with the bowline.

Jessica noted with satisfaction that while she hadn't caused any lasting romantic effects, her withdrawal hadn't helped his mood. She rubbed the side of her nose absently and leaned over to fasten the stern line without reply.

Cal's jaw tightened even more when he came back to see the neat half-hitch she'd dropped over the cleat. He vaulted to the dock and reached down to help her onto the pier without commenting.

Jessica straightened beside him and pretended to survey herself with amazement. "Golly—I *am* improving. I should manage to get back unscathed unless I take a header off the pier." She looked up at his unsmiling face. "Thank you for the . . . ride."

"Look, Jess . . ." He put a detaining hand on her forearm when she would have turned away. "I've been thinking. We'd better have a longer talk, after all. There's no reason why—"

"Cal, darling—you're early. What a lovely surprise!" Valerie's happy tones sent them apart as effectively as if a machete had landed at their feet. Jessica started to take a step backward until she remembered that the first step—while not a long one—certainly would be deep. Cal must have been reading her mind again because his arm came out automatically and clamped onto her elbow.

"I wish you'd told me you were going out this morning," Valerie said to him, managing a "poor-little-me" tone. "Probably I could have arranged to get away—after all the overtime I've been logging." She sidled up and took his other arm in a possessive gesture. "It doesn't matter though, darling. I'll forgive you if you buy me a late lunch."

"I've already had lunch," Cal began, and then grimaced in surrender at her crestfallen expression. "Okay. At least we can have dessert or something."

While seething inwardly over his change of mind, Jessica had to acknowledge it would have been a hard-hearted man to withstand Valerie in her outfit of red shorts and peppermint-striped shirt. The shirt buttons didn't serve any functional purpose until almost her waist, and the expanse of visible skin almost defeated the temptation to gaze at her long tanned legs. Almost, but not quite, Jessica noted as Cal considered the view. For an instant, she thought of asking the secretary how many times she changed clothes each day, and then gave herself a mental jab. There was no use dwelling on such unimportant things.

Fortunately she was ready with a reply when Cal turned to her and said, "You'll join us, of course, Jessica?"

Jessica had a moment to enjoy the sudden frown that crossed Valerie's features before she shook her head. "I really can't, thanks. This may be a vacation for you, but I have some things to accomplish before I go back to Texas. Thanks for the sail, though—and that time we spent in the cove." She let her voice drop seductively and managed a quick nuzzle against his chest. "Let's do it again soon."

Her eyes were gleaming with mischief when she looked up. Her glee faded abruptly as Cal put a lean finger under her chin and kept her face turned to his. "Oh, we will, love," he said in a tone that showed he knew exactly what her game was and he wasn't particularly amused. "Sooner than you think. Take care." With the careless injunction, he bestowed a decidedly thorough kiss on her parted lips.

When he finally released her, it was all she could do to keep upright and not have to hang on to the signboard beside her, which warned boaters of all the dangers on the pier. Unfortunately they had overlooked the six-foot tall one standing beside her, Jessica thought as she tried to get her breathing back in sequence.

"Need any help?" Cal was watching her with a wry expression.

Jessica managed to say levelly, "Certainly not. I'm perfectly fine. It just takes a little while to get my land legs back again." She took another deep breath and headed for the center of the wooden dock, adding over her shoulder, "I'll see you later—one place or another."

"Really, Cal—she takes a lot for granted." Valerie's voice was shrill in protest a moment later, loud enough so that Jessica didn't have any trouble hearing it, even though she was halfway up the dock by then. Unfortunately Cal's reply must have been at a lower pitch or she was beyond range. Jessica walked purposefully onward as if she really had a destination in mind and couldn't wait to get there.

She didn't slow her pace until she reached the street bordering the hillside. Only when she finally rounded the corner onto Main Street did she allow herself the luxury of sitting down on a low stone wall erected to keep a rock garden from slithering onto the sidewalk.

If she were to keep her pride intact, she couldn't slink back to the apartment and appear to be waiting for Cal's return whenever he decided to quit Valerie's eager grasp. On the other hand, it was hard to dream up a busy social schedule when she didn't know anyone in town. The closest Friday Harbor had to a singles' bar was the lounge of the popular restaurant on the waterfront, which didn't open until dark— even if she'd been in the mood to patronize it. Of course, she could always accost one of the departing passengers from the ferry. Her lips twitched with laughter as she visualized the reaction she'd get if she sidled up to the solemn professorial type she saw striding up the block just then. All she'd have to do was murmur, "How long you going to be in town, mister?" to send him fleeing back to the ferry dock. Either that or he'd have a heart attack on the spot.

Jessica watched the man cross the street, intent on a display of fishing tackle in the sporting-goods store. "He'll never know what a narrow escape he had," she murmured under her breath, and then shook her head. She *was* in a bad way. Talking to herself, and cold sober in the bargain. She stood up, deciding to walk along Main Street too. At least she could window-shop while she tried to think of a more worthwhile project.

In the second block, she came upon the real-estate office where she'd encountered Bruce Lightner and Cal, and she pulled up to gaze at the display window. Her glance was ostensibly on the colored placards with pictured homes and prices of the island real estate, but her thoughts were with Cal and Valerie, wondering where their late lunch was going to take place.

"Anything I can persuade you to buy? We've more listings that aren't pictured in the window."

Jessica gave a nervous start and glanced around to see a young man in his twenties, casually dressed in a long-sleeved sport shirt and jeans, who was apprais-ing her cheerfully.

"It's okay, I work here," he went on, noting her involuntary withdrawal. "It would sure help my ca-reer if I could make a sale while my boss is away."

"Your boss?"

"Yeah, Mr. Lightner." His expression became thoughtful. "I thought everybody in town knew who he was."

"They probably do," Jessica acknowledged with a smile. "I'm not one of the natives."

"I didn't really think you were. They don't waste much time looking in our window—they'd be inside signing papers to put the old family home on the market. I'm Judd Harley, and you're . . ." He paused significantly.

"Jessica Webster," she admitted. "And I wouldn't worry about your career in salesmanship. Something tells me you'll do very well."

He leaned against the window to gaze at her appreciatively. "We should really discuss it over coffee, but right now I'm holding down the office." He ran his fingers through his thick fair hair as another thought occurred to him. "Tell you what! I'll turn on the answering machine and take you out to look at some properties. That way, nobody will have any complaints." As Jessica started to shake her head, he went on in an earnest tone, "You don't have to worry—we could drive past some of the better listings if you'll tell me what you had in mind."

Jessica decided quickly that Judd wasn't the person she'd choose if she decided to list her family's property, but on the other hand, it might not hurt to learn the local gossip about the fire. "I can't afford much of anything right now," she told him. "Maybe someday, though." At his crestfallen look, she decided to risk her theory. "I'd always hoped for a weekend place out by English Camp."

"That part of the island doesn't come cheap," Judd replied, falling quickly into his salesman's role. "You'd do better closer to town. Then you could rent to the locals in the off-season to help with the payments. There's an old place that could do with some fixing-up . . . about a half-mile away."

"A handyman's delight?" Jessica's tone was ironic.

"No, thanks. I'm fresh out of handymen and my talent is limited to a hammer and screwdriver."

Judd twirled an imaginary mustache. "Something tells me that you'd have a volunteer labor pool once the word got round. I'm pretty good at fixing things up myself."

"I'll remember if I change my mind," she said, resisting an urge to tell him to try his talents on the local women.

"At least, we could take a look." He glanced at his watch. "Two more hours before I finish my shift, and Bruce won't like it if I spend the time polishing ashtrays."

"I'm not much of a prospect," she warned.

"You're warm and breathing. And beautiful," he added with an air of discovery. He patted her shoulder as he went on rapidly, "Just stay here while I set the answering machine. Be back in a tick. My car's parked right down the block. Okay?"

He went back into the real-estate office before Jessica could decide on an answer. She lingered on the threshold, chewing her bottom lip uncertainly. It was stupid to spend the rest of the afternoon with a real-estate salesman that she didn't even know. Granted, he was a fairly attractive man, but somehow she wasn't in the mood for enlarging her social circle just then.

On the verge of going in the office and issuing a definite "no" to Judd's invitation, she hesitated again—acknowledging that the only reason she was even considering it was to give Cal Sloane something to think about. She'd be an utter fool to hang around waiting for him to reappear, Jessica reminded herself, and sighed as Judd bounded out the door, stopping just long enough to position a "Closed" sign on it.

"All set?" he inquired, catching her hand in a possessive grip and steering her down the sidewalk.

"All set," she agreed, trying to put some enthusiasm in her tone while she wondered why in hell she was so weak-minded.

"Great! My car's just down this way. At least at this time of year we don't have to worry about finding a parking space on Main Street. One of the many advantages of being a permanent resident," he told her with a grin.

"I'll remember," she promised. She could have told him that her family ties to the island could probably put his to shame, but resisted the temptation. "Which way do we go first?" she asked as he pulled up beside an expensive sports car and unlocked the door with a flourish.

He looked daunted for a moment—clearly he'd hoped for some sign that she was impressed with her mode of transportation. Then he shrugged and said, "I thought we'd go along the shore on the south side first. That way, I can convince Bruce that we weren't just out joyriding."

Jessica decided to take pity on him. "We'd be lying, though, wouldn't we?" She patted the elegant dashboard and smiled as he slid behind the wheel. "I didn't expect to be transported in such style."

Judd's shoulders went back and he raked his fingers through his hair. "It's a nice set of wheels," he admitted.

"I'm definitely impressed," she said, trying to sound as if she meant it.

"Yeah—well, we'd better be off before the 'powers that be' come back on the scene." He started the engine with a roar loud enough to make a man walking by on the sidewalk jump and shoot an annoyed look in their direction.

Jessica tried to pretend that she hadn't noticed and hung on as Judd reversed out of the parking space with a jerk. "I thought you'd said that your boss wouldn't be back this afternoon."

"Sometimes he changes his mind. It doesn't matter now—we're out of range," Judd said, barely hesitating at the intersection before turning left and accelerating.

They were able to go only two blocks before Judd braked violently to let a young mother wheel a stroller across the street. Jessica hid a smile as he swore under his breath; the conditions weren't great for a driver attempting Grand Prix maneuvers. After another block or two, he gave up his showy gestures as they reached the crest of the hill where the homes had a splendid view of the channel below. "Water view keeps the price up on these," Judd said, adopting a professional tone as he gestured toward a "For Sale" sign at the roadside.

"How much?" Jessica asked with real interest, and let out a silent whistle when he told her. "There's definitely gold in these hills."

"That's because the Californians have decided to head north, since their real estate's so expensive," he said, speeding up again. "They figure it's only a matter of a few years till we'll match the price here in the San Juans. You're sure you can't scratch up a down payment?"

"Quite sure," she told him, crossing her fingers out of sight.

"Well, in that case," he said with a quick sideways grin, "I can stop being official. How about a nice ride out to American Camp?"

"I'll leave it up to you," she said, leaning back in the seat.

"That's what I like to hear. We'll start at the end of the island and then maybe loop down to the other part."

"Perfect. Would there be time to take in English Camp too? There's some pretty scenery down that way, isn't there?"

He nodded, clearly more interested in the way his car was performing than clinging to his role of real-estate salesman. "Not much on the market around there, though. A lot of people want to be close to Friday Harbor. The natives have to think about commuting on the ferry, so we don't have many listings in that part of the island."

"Well, since I'm not a real prospect, it doesn't matter. I'm glad the fog lifted today so that we can go sightseeing."

"And maybe take a break down at Roche Harbor?" Judd asked hopefully.

"If you won't get in trouble goofing off."

His grin appeared again. "We're the only ones who know the score on that."

She held her palm up and said solemnly, "The secret's safe with me, mister."

He erupted with sudden laughter. "Then next stop American Camp. Hang on."

The warning was timely because he accelerated on a straight stretch and then slammed on the brakes when they came up behind a farm tractor after rounding a curve. Judd swore under his breath and Jessica clung to the door handle beside her. When they'd maneuvered around the tractor and increased speed again, she found herself wondering if she'd make it back to Friday Harbor in a vertical position.

Judd must have noticed the tight set of her jaw because he lowered his speed when they finally came upon the signboard for American Camp, and made an effort to charm her into a more relaxed mood. "Do you know your history about the pig war?" he asked as they drove past some of the old garrisons from the American occupation of the island in 1859. "Or would you like a blow-by-blow account?"

Jessica had been weaned on the story of the squabble that followed the shooting of a pig on the island. "I know that there was a confrontation between American and British troops, but fortunately the commanding officers kept their heads."

"Yeah, but not until almost five hundred Americans were opposed by five British warships carrying over two thousand British troops. When the politicians back in Washington, D.C., caught word of it, the fur really flew." Judd pulled to a stop on the edge of the gravel track and indicated the remnants of the buildings which had housed the American forces. "When you think that it happened barely a hundred years ago, it strikes a lot closer to home than just an item in the history books."

"I'm surprised that nobody has erected a statue for that unfortunate pig who was the only casualty."

"There weren't any protest groups for animal rights in those days," he said, grinning.

"So it seems." She looked at the peaceful countryside around them, where the only sign of activity was a power cruiser far below, heading south toward the main channel. "Hard to believe that the soldiers stayed on the island in joint occupation for twelve whole years."

"I'll bet that everybody kept their livestock penned up tight all the time," he agreed. He shifted into gear and pulled onto the deserted road again. "Let's forget the history angle and find something more interesting." He gave her a rueful sideways glance as he asked, "How did we get stuck in the past, anyhow?"

"History is hard to ignore on San Juan. That isn't why I want to visit English Camp, though. It's supposed to one of the prettiest spots on the island."

Judd slowed as they reached an intersection where he could head back the way they'd come. "Then you've seen the place?"

"Actually, not for a while," she admitted. Certainly she didn't intend to say just how recently it had been. Probably it would have been smarter to drive her own car, but if she could convince Judd that they were on a sightseeing trip, it would work just as well. "If we stop for coffee at Roche Harbor, the English Camp won't really be out of our way, will it?" She managed a wistful tone and hoped she sounded properly submissive.

Apparently her strategy worked, because he patted her reassuringly on the knee. "Not a bit. Besides, I left word for Bruce not to expect me back this afternoon." His tone turned smug as he added, "I'll bet that we can find something more interesting than a cup of coffee when we get to Roche. We have a couple of condos for sale there and I just happen to have the keys."

Jessica's stomach muscles tightened at this announcement. Clearly she'd have to make a move before she found herself in a deserted condominium while Judd tried out another kind of salesmanship. On the other hand, there was plenty of time after they viewed English Camp to devise a convincing reason why she had to get back to Friday Harbor without delay.

Conversation dropped to mere essentials after that.

Judd seemed content to enjoy his driving, tossing in a few Grand Prix maneuvers whenever he could, but not enough that Jessica had to clutch the edge of her seat very often. When they arrived at English Camp and found the parking lot completely deserted, she didn't know whether to be relieved or not.

Judd pulled up with his usual flourish and left the engine idling long enough to ask, "Sure you want to spend any time here? It's a long walk down to the beach, and just a bunch of scenery when you get there."

"I know"—Jessica reached determinedly for her door handle—"but I want to see that garden again. You know, the one the English planted to remind them of home."

"Okay." Judd's consent was grudging and it was obvious that he had hoped for better things as he turned off the ignition and opened his door. "Don't blame me if there's nothing but a lot of dead plants at this time of year. Hey, wait up."

Jessica threw him a brief smile over her shoulder, but she didn't slow her steps as she set out for the steep trail leading down the hill.

"Anybody would think you were running the anchor leg of a relay," Judd complained as he caught up so that they could walk abreast. "We're not in that much of a hurry—even though I am anxious to get to Roche." He managed a satisfied smirk, which didn't help his cause, since Jessica was keeping her attention on the quiet water beyond the bottom of the path.

"There don't seem to be any boats in the channel," she muttered, unable to keep the disappointment from her voice.

"I'm not surprised. It's late in the year for pleasure cruising, and this part of the island is off the main track. It's mainly local traffic out there," he added, sounding slightly impatient. "Besides, I thought you just wanted to see that garden." He motioned toward the white-picket-fence enclosure that she'd mentioned as an excuse.

"I do. I mean, I did," she said vaguely, and then gestured at the entire settlement. "Everybody says this is the most picturesque part of the island."

He shrugged as they reached the bottom of the path and started across the grass meadow abutting the water. "If you like to read historical signs and stare at a few deserted houses, I guess you're right. Frankly, I prefer more action when I go sightseeing."

Jessica shot him an uneasy glance from under half-closed lids, wondering if he were idiotic enough to make a pass in the deserted English Camp. For the first time, she became aware of how really alone they were at the historical site and wished that a busload of tourists would suddenly descend from the parking lot above. Since there didn't seem to be any possibility of that, she tried another maneuver that might work to cool any ardor on his part.

She dragged a handkerchief from her purse just in time to mop up after a resounding sneeze. "Terribly sorry," she muttered into its folds. "I must be starting a miserable cold. It can't be hay fever at this time of year, although my sinuses were really playing up this morning. Do you have any trouble that way?" she asked, trying to throw herself into the hypochondriac role with gusto.

As she hoped, Judd's features twisted with distaste before he rearranged them again. "Not so you could notice," he said. He watched her rub the end of her nose before adding impatiently, "Seen enough of the garden yet?"

Jessica walked past the huge tree which bordered it and stared at the flowerbeds inside the enclosure. As he'd warned, other than a few evergreens, there wasn't much to see. As idly as possible, she let her glance move on toward her own property, where a concrete foundation was all that remained of the burned-out house. The beach in front of it where Cal had been lying the night before was empty too, with only a few strands of seaweed littering the rocky shore.

"All done and over," she quoted softly.

"What did you say?" Judd asked.

"Nothing. Nothing at all." Her gaze moved on up the empty waterway and she felt a sudden surge of disappointment. Somehow she'd thought to catch a glimpse of the big sailboat that had been headed that way earlier in the day. "It's so quiet," she murmured. "I'd forgotten how 'out of this world' the island can be."

"Most people come for that very thing," Judd said, shoving his hands in his pockets. "As a matter of fact, that's one of the selling points that Bruce keeps harping on. You're the only one I've ever heard complain."

"I'm not really complaining—"

He cut her off with an impatient wave of his hand. "Believe me, I understand. If I had a choice, I sure as hell would get off the island to find some action." He kicked a pebble at the side of the path for emphasis and then checked his watch. "Whatcha say we get going? Otherwise there won't be enough time to enjoy our next stop." He caught her hand and gave it an encouraging squeeze. "There's no reason we can't salvage a little enjoyment from the afternoon."

Jessica's initial impulse was to yank her fingers from his clasp, but she managed to restrain herself and turn with him back toward the path—all the while casting about for a reason to cut their expedition short. A headache was such a hackneyed excuse that she dismissed it immediately, although the prospect of much more time in Judd's company was turning the threat into a reality. Halfway up the path, she debated the possibility of a turned ankle, but it was hard to fake, since the biggest rocks in sight along the trail could have been used for bird gravel. So scratch the turned ankle, she thought unhappily.

They had reached the top of the hill and Judd had taken a proprietary grip on her elbow to steer her toward the car when help came from an unexpected source.

"What did you say?" he asked, startled into stopping in the midst of a curving exit drive.

"Nothing," she retorted. "I didn't . . ." There was a distinct pause while she hiccuped resoundingly. "I didn't say anything."

"You hiccuped." It wasn't so much a statement as an accusation.

"So, I hiccuped," she agreed, and then did it again to prove it wasn't a fluke. "It happens once in a while," she said, suddenly seeing an end to her troubles. No man, even one starved for female company, would dally with a woman who was hiccuping every thirty seconds.

"Hey! What d'ya know!"

Judd's exclamation brought her head around quickly. Just in time to see his disgruntled expression as she hiccuped again. "Hell!" he muttered, reaching in his pocket for the car keys. "I thought you were over them."

For a panic-stricken moment Jessica had thought

the same thing, and determined that it wouldn't happen again. At least, until they were back within the city limits of Friday Harbor. "I'm sorry," she said, trying to sound properly disappointed as she climbed into the car. "It usually takes me a long time to get over them. You might say I'm a chronic case." She waited until he'd gotten behind the wheel and slammed his door with more force than necessary. "There was a time last year when they lasted all weekend. Of course, my doctor was out of town, so it was a case of wondering whether to try the emergency room at the hospital or—"

Her words were cut off as Judd accelerated so fast out of the parking lot that she almost had a real case of whiplash to go with the imaginary hiccups. She waited until they'd joined the main road back to Friday Harbor before she said, "I'm terribly sorry that this has to spoil the rest of the afternoon," between two carefully spaced hiccups.

"I'll live," Judd grated out, his jaw tight with annoyance. "I don't suppose that you want a drink now. Unless"—he gave her a quick sideways glance— "you think it might do a quick cure."

"Oh, no," Jessica replied quickly, before he could enlarge that possibility. "This sort of thing makes me nauseous too. Nerves, I suppose." She waved a feeble hand hoping to convey that she might have to take to her bed in short order.

"Ummph." Judd's grunt reassured her that if there were any bed in question, she'd definitely be occupying it alone. Hypochondriacs weren't in his scheme of things. "Was there anything that interested you in the real-estate market?" he commented after a mile or two of silence. "It wouldn't hurt to let Bruce think that I had a live one on the line—so the afternoon won't be a total waste."

Jessica winced, although she couldn't really blame him for feeling the way he did. "I wish I could promise something," she said between carefully timed hiccups. "Unfortunately I can't afford any of the houses on the water, and a vacant lot would have me bankrupt paying taxes. You can tell your boss that I was mildly interested in the English Camp area if you think that would help."

"There isn't anything for sale out there."

Jessica decided to probe a little deeper into the real-estate scuttlebutt on the island. "There was sort of a burned-out foundation just beyond the garden area," she said, keeping her voice casual between hiccups. "Is there any chance of a fire-sale price on a place like that?"

"S'funny you should ask about that," he commented after an instant or two. "There've been a couple of inquiries about the place recently."

"Probably people like me, wanting to pick up a bargain below the going rate."

He made a noncommittal grunt. "Then you've got another think coming. It's a nice spread of waterfront—that's all that counts around here."

"You mean that it *is* on the market?" Jessica was aghast at this newest revelation.

"I've heard that it might be. Say, you must be feeling better." Then, as Jessica managed a hurried hiccup, he went on. "At least, you're thinking about something besides what's wrong with you."

"I'm sorry if I bored you," she said, trying for a quaver in her voice. "Actually a person can't help something . . . er . . . physical."

"I guess it's a change from a headache," Judd replied, showing that she hadn't been all that convincing. "Do you mind if I drop you off at my office when we get back in town?"

He didn't sound as if he cared one way or the other. Definitely a case of "here's your hat and what's your hurry," Jessica thought even as she said, "The office will be fine."

"I'm sorry that I have other plans for dinner," Judd told her.

"Really, it's perfectly all right." Jessica didn't have any trouble sounding sincere that time, since she was counting the minutes until she could get out of his sight.

"Well, if you're sure. It's going to be dark pretty soon." He gestured at the fading shadows by the roadside as they cleared a grove of trees. "At this time of year—" He broke off to wave at the driver of a car which passed them coming from town, but didn't slacken speed.

"Friend of yours?"

"Val?" he replied automatically, and then shot her a hooded glance. "You mean that woman in the car?" At Jessica's nod, he shrugged and returned his attention to the road in front of them. "Just an acquaintance. She lives here year-round. This is a small place so it doesn't take long to size up who's available."

"And she is?"

"You might say so. At least that's the rumor around town. Personally I wouldn't know. Why?"

"No reason. I just thought she looked familiar."

"You can find her at the Institute. That sounds like a bad song title, doesn't it? North Pacific Marine Institute," he added impatiently when Jessica didn't respond. "It's the think tank on the edge of town. You must have seen the place if you came in on the ferry. Or at least heard about it. They get plenty of publicity about their research on whales. As if anybody cared."

"I think some people do," Jessica put in mildly.

"Not enough to beef up their budget—that's the trouble right now." Judd lowered his speed as they approached a stop sign at the edge of town. "Valerie and a lot of others will be out on the sidewalk if there isn't an appropriation of state money to bail them out. It couldn't happen to a nicer bunch."

Jessica kept her tone casual. "You sound a little bitter."

"Maybe with good reason. Madame Valerie is due for a fall. I heard that she bet on the wrong horse not long ago and now she's out trying her luck again."

Jessica tried to hurriedly sort through his innuendos to decide whether he was just serving up the latest town gossip or whether there was a basis in fact. It certainly put a new angle on the woman's determined pursuit of Cal Sloane. She remembered a quick hiccup before saying, "This place sounds like every other small town. Your neighbors know what's happening before you do."

"Oh, I wouldn't say that. Sometimes a small town is the perfect cover."

"You mean you have a secret life that would shock the town elders?"

He snorted with amusement. "This afternoon was a good example of my red-hot social life. Valerie might have an item or two to pass on, but . . ." His words trailed off.

"Who knows?" Jessica decided that it was a good time to end the discussion before he started sulking again over the way his day had turned out. "Would you please drop me off in front of the Park Department? I want to pick up a couple of brochures and a map of the island."

He glanced at his watch as they turned into the main street of town and headed toward the dock area. "They may have already closed. Besides, I need to get some more information from you—you know, local address and telephone number, that sort of stuff. I have to fill out a prospect card for my boss."

Despite those objections, he was braking in front of the National Park office at the end of the block and Jessica reached for her door handle. "Don't worry—I can drop in tomorrow and fill out the necessary forms. Tell Mr. Lightner that I was a little under the weather and wanted to go lie down."

Judd eyed her derisively. "Too bad we couldn't have had the same idea at the same time. You must be feeling better—at least your hiccups seem to have disappeared."

"So they have. I hope it lasts." She got out of the car and turned to face him before closing the door. "Thanks again for the ride."

"I'll see you tomorrow." Judd sounded definite about that.

Not if I see you first, Jessica thought. Aloud she said, "I'll do my best to get in touch. Thanks again." That time, she closed the door firmly and headed toward the Park Department doorway just down the sidewalk. Behind her, she heard the squeal of tires as Judd let her know that he wasn't happy with her last words. Jessica deliberately kept her glance on the buildings in case he was checking on her in the rear-vision mirror, and she heaved a sigh of relief when she was sure that the car was out of sight.

As Judd had warned, the Park Department offices

wee closed for the day, but she wasted another two or three minutes in the doorway until she felt it was safe to walk to the end of the block and head for the condominium. She wasn't sure exactly what tack she was going to take with Cal when she met him again, but she couldn't waste any more time delaying that encounter.

She managed to thread her way through the parked cars waiting to board the ferry at the dock, and then walked down the concrete path to the condominium. It wouldn't be long until dark, she thought, and wished suddenly that she could be looking forward to a nice quiet evening with Cal in front of the fireplace in the apartment. Even if they argued all night—as they probably would.

The prospect was so appealing that it took a moment or two for her to realize that the darkened windows of her condo meant that there was still nobody at home. Jessica paused at the bottom of the stairs and checked the upper condominium, whose darkened windows showed that Cal hadn't moved upstairs yet. There could still be a note on her living-room table saying, "Thanks for the hospitality, see you around." Considering the way they'd parted, she couldn't expect much more.

She felt a little better five minutes later when a quick search of her deserted condo showed nary a note and Cal's baggage still in the front bedroom. Even his damp traveler's checks were drying on top of the bureau.

Another couple of minutes wandering through the empty rooms and peering into the stark interior of the refrigerator brought the frown back to her face. She wasn't in the mood for solitude—although during her afternoon with Judd, she would have happily traded half a month's salary for just such an existence.

She hiccuped absently at the memory and said, "Oh, my God!" at the thought that she might actually have triggered some real ones.

There was a muffled noise nearby and she paused in her survey of the kitchen to look warily around. Whatever had brushed against her ankles early in the morning might very well be lurking behind the refrigerator or the washing machine just a few feet away. Without thinking, she hiccuped again and then said loudly, "That does it!"

She walked toward the front door, catching up a sweater on the way. Dinner at the local fast-food outlet might not be great for her digestion but it certainly would be healthier than sitting in an empty condo and building up symptoms for the local shrink.

The waterfront path was now dimly lit by bulbs concealed in the grass edging, but the muted, sporadic rattle of some metal gear made her glance over her shoulder. Her gaze narrowed as she saw the outlines of Bruce Lightner's big sailboat tied up at the dock. Evidently his cruise had been a short one and he'd since gone on to other things. Like checking on Judd's afternoon sales, she thought with a wry grin as she walked toward the lighted street.

She saw that her rented car was in its proper stall at the carport but decided against driving the short distance uptown. The restaurant was only a few blocks away and one good thing about Friday Harbor was that its sidewalks were still safe for nighttime strolling.

Fifteen minutes later Jessica was collecting her hamburger and fries and searching for an empty table by the window overlooking the ferry dock. She had cast an apprehensive glance around the restaurant before ordering her food to make sure that there weren't any familiar faces. Not that she would have retreated if she'd encountered Cal, but that hope faded fast after counting noses.

It was disturbing that her thoughts kept returning to him as she munched her way through dinner. Certainly she knew better. If she had any sense, she would have concentrated on the plethora of small yachts homing into the empty moorages in the marina and the groups of people wandering along the broad public dock, which was the only brilliantly lit area on view.

She glanced at her watch when she left the restaurant later on and shook her head in disbelief. Only forty minutes had passed despite her tarrying over a second cup of coffee and an ice-cream sundae. It certainly wasn't late enough to convince Cal that she'd spent a riotous afternoon and evening on the town.

The lighted marquee of the small movie house on the main street made her pause at the street corner and survey it thoughtfully. The feature wasn't bad—she'd been meaning to see it on the first run and then had decided that she'd rent the video version. This would be just as good, and since it looked as if the performance had already started, she could slip in the back row and leave before the lights came on again so that her attendance would go unobserved.

She had forgotten only one thing in her plans and that was the refreshment stand in the lobby. As she was handing her ticket to the boy at the door, she caught a glimpse of Judd there collecting a big box of buttered popcorn. He lingered, putting his change in his pants pocket before he pushed aside the curtain that separated the movie section.

Jessica waited long enough for the curtain to fall into place and then followed him to make sure that she didn't sit in the seat alongside.

As she stood at the rear of the theater to allow her eyes to get used to the darkness, she saw that she needn't have worried. Judd slid into an aisle seat just a half-dozen rows down and was offering the popcorn to his date of the evening. Jessica slipped into a place in the back row and tried to assimilate what she'd just seen. After all his comments about Valerie Long when they'd passed on the highway, he'd gone straight out and made a date with her for the evening!

As the feature progressed, Jessica noted that the box of popcorn wasn't the only thing they were sharing. There was more than an ordinary amount of chitchat, and at one point Judd put his arm around her shoulders and Valerie seemed content to have it there.

Jessica was watching the two of them so closely that time passed faster than she expected. She got up from her seat reluctantly as the music for the final chase sequence rose to a crescendo. She stayed in the tiny lobby for an instant, wishing she dared wait and see where the two of them were bound. Then she decided against it as the lights flickered on inside the theater.

She didn't waste any time after that, hurrying down the short distance to the end of the block. As she turned the corner, she glanced over her shoulder and noticed that some theater patrons were straggling out, but Judd and Valerie weren't in sight.

Jessica sighed in relief and strolled the rest of the way down toward the condominium block while her thoughts stayed on the strange twosome. Or was it strange after all? Even a short time with Judd showed that he wasn't particular about which woman he had in tow—just so he had one. "And she's welcome to him," Jessica murmured as she passed the carport for the condo and made her way to the sheltered path behind the buildings.

The dim spotlights placed at intervals along the edge of the walk were welcome, she decided, treading carefully to avoid the slippery fallen leaves on the concrete. Strange how much darker it seemed at the island than in the suburbs of a city. And how much quieter, she thought as the sound of her footsteps cut through the still night air.

Her sudden shiver didn't have anything to do with the temperature. It was imagination again, she told herself fiercely, and kept walking almost as fast as before.

A sudden sound of metal crashing against metal cleaved through the quiet evening and brought her to an abrupt stop. She glanced around the dark pathway, knowing that the sound hadn't come from the landscaped beds to her right or the back of the condominium building to her left. She remained frozen in place, and then, when nothing happened, she carefully moved forward.

This time, however, she walked along the grass at the edge of the path so that her presence wouldn't be quite so evident. When she came to the end of the building, she almost tiptoed around the corner.

She frowned as she surveyed the darkened boats at their pier, knowing that she'd expected to find some activity at the waterside. Then, as she half-turned to go up the steps of her own condo, a strange whine reached her ears. She stopped again—sure that the noise had come from one of the anchored boats.

This time, persistence paid off as she caught a

glimpse of light behind a porthole on the big sailboat. Of course! It wasn't a human whine she'd heard, she told herself—it was the German shepherd that belonged to Bruce Lightner. Bruce must keep him aboard as a watchdog.

Jessica's thoughts raced as she stood at the deserted stair and tried to peer through the darkness toward the boat. The whine came again and then was abruptly cut off—as if someone aboard had made sure of it. On the other hand, there was the possibility that it wasn't an animal whimper. Perhaps some person aboard was hurt and needed help.

Jessica chewed on her lower lip and said, "Damn! Damn! Damn!" in a fervent undertone as she wondered what to do.

The safest, most sensible, adult thing was to walk up the stairs, unlock the door to her apartment, and go inside. "Just like an ostrich," Jessica muttered again. "Then I'd never know what happened. There's a chance that somebody could die if I follow that philosophy."

They were hard words and did what she intended them to do—stiffened her backbone, which was jellylike in parts. It got more so when the path lights which were her only source of illumination suddenly went out.

Jessica drew a sharp breath and tried to distinguish shapes in the dark. At least she could go a little closer to the boat. Then, if there were something that smacked of an emergency, she could hurry up to the condo and phone the authorities.

The conviction that she'd figured out the right thing to do made her edge closer to Bruce's vessel. The moon was under a cloud cover just then, but she still sought safety in the foliage of a huge rhododendron planted near the pier.

She was so intent on her task that the sound of footsteps behind her registered far too late to take evasive action.

All she knew was that a big black figure emerged like a specter from the gloom and she saw an arm reaching out for her as she drew in her breath to scream.

Then, horribly, a hand covered her mouth. Her desperate shriek changed to a suffocating gurgle even as another arm came around her shoulders and pulled her backward.

Jessica knew she was falling but that was the last conscious thought to register. Sheer terror wiped out everything else and, too late, the pale moon emerged from its cloud cover to shine down on her still, crumpled form, half-hidden in the shrubbery.

From the water, the whine sounded again. There was a muffled curse before silence settled on the scene—broken only by the lapping of waves against the bulkhead.

6

When Jessica opened her eyes again, she blinked at the sudden light and then frowned as she tried to make sense of her surroundings.

Gone were the marina, the shrubbery, certainly the darkness and gloom. Her frown deepened as the rest suddenly came flooding back: the terrifying figure—the hand that covered her face—

She struggled to sit up and asked, "What happened?" Then, sounding slightly stronger, "Where am I?"

"I'd really expected something more original," said Cal's voice from the vicinity of her shoulder. "Where in the hell does it look like?"

Jessica tried to focus on her surroundings. "Your bedroom . . . I mean, my bedroom . . . or . . ."

"Okay, okay. We'll take it as read. There's no need to go into the legal ownership right now." He sat down on the edge of the mattress beside her. "How do you feel?"

He put the question in a much more diffident tone than his other comments, and Jessica noticed for the first time that he was holding a washcloth. Her hand went up to her damp forehead and her forefinger traced a rivulet still coursing her cheek. "How did I . . . ?" Somehow even the simplest question seemed beyond her then, and she had to start again. She indicated the washcloth and asked, "That was for me?"

Cal stirred slightly on the bed and frowned at the cloth as if wondering what to do with it. "Yes. Well, it seemed like a good idea. You were a hell of a long time coming out of that faint," he added, sounding exasperated again. "Now, if you're up to it, I'll get you to a doctor. Probably I should have done that in the first place, but I wasn't thinking straight. I'll try to carry you to the car—it'll probably be faster than waiting for a house call. Or do doctors even make house calls in Friday Harbor?"

Jessica hoisted herself to a sitting position against the headboard of the bed. "I haven't the faintest idea and I don't intend to find out. There's nothing really wrong with me. Some creep came up behind me and scared me to death. That's when I must have collapsed into the shrubbery—" Her words stopped as she saw Cal stare fixedly at the floor. "Wait a minute!" She swiped absently at another drop of water that was just about to leave her jawbone. "Were you . . . I mean, did you—"

He interrupted her stammerings. "I was and I did. I'm sorry about scaring you. That wasn't intentional. Although at the time, I could have cheerfully throttled you." Hearing her sudden indrawn breath, he drawled, "Don't worry, your throat's still intact. Probably in a hell of a lot better shape than my blood pressure after having you draped over my arm in the bushes."

As an apology, Jessica felt that it left a lot to be desired. "I can tell that you're really crestfallen. Next

you'll be complaining about straining your back when
you hauled me up the stairs."

"Now that you mention it . . ." Cal rubbed his
side and then managed a reluctant grin. "Okay. I'm a
dirty dog and my manners leave a lot to be desired.
On the other hand," he went on when she would have
interrupted, "you have an amazing talent for turning
up precisely at the wrong time."

"Good Lord! All I did was walk home from the
movies," she flared.

"Lurking in the rhododendrons doesn't fit that de-
scription, unless you've taken up bird-watching or
stargazing for your late nights."

"Not exactly." Jessica hesitated for a moment, wondering how much to confess, and then, as another
thought suddenly struck her, she switched to the
offensive. "Apparently I'm not the only stargazer.
There must have been two of us crouching in that
same rhododendron." She drew herself up straighter
against the pillow. "What in the dickens were you
doing there? And don't tell me you'd stopped to
smell the flowers along the way. You're not the type."

"You haven't got the foggiest idea in hell of what
type I am," he said with some amusement.

"Oh, I don't know . . ." Her eyes narrowed. "I'm
not following that red herring. What *were* you doing
out there? Besides scaring me out of my senses?"

"I told you—"

"I know—I know," she interrupted him ruthlessly.
"It was all a great big mistake."

"Not exactly. I hoped to get you out of the way
without completely lousing up my surveillance.
Unfortunately"—he shrugged and got up off the
bed—"it didn't work out that way."

"Because I fainted?"

"That's right. I may not be Sir Galahad, but I'm still not programmed to leave a woman nuzzling the dandelions."

"Why didn't you leave me alone in the first place? I wasn't trotting around the neighborhood with a tambourine, if you'll remember."

"There's nothing wrong with my memory." Cal leaned against the door frame and fixed her with a piercing glance. "Knowing you, the next step would have been to investigate what was happening aboard. Am I right?"

For an instant Jessica thought about trying to brazen it out, and then she decided she wasn't up to it. While she certainly didn't need the doctor's visit that Cal had advocated, she was far from fighting fit. She blinked in surprise as she saw him approach the bed again. "What's the matter?"

"That's what I want to know. Are you sure you're all right?" he asked, putting a cool palm on her forehead.

"Of course I am." Jessica stayed very still so as not to dislodge it. "Why do you ask?"

"Because you didn't answer my question." Then, straightening again, he stared down at her. "Do you remember what we were talking about?"

"Certainly I do." Color rose in her cheeks as she realized that she was busy plotting an alibi that she'd ignored the important part. "You wanted to know if I was going to board Bruce's sailboat."

Relief erased the frown as he went back to stand in the doorway. "Well, you've had long enough to figure out an answer. Why don't we take it from the top for a change."

Jessica ignored his sarcasm. "I really hadn't made up my mind. I was trying to figure out what the noise was—if it had turned out to be his German shepherd, I wasn't keen on a head-to-head confrontation. Or is it fang-to-fang?"

Cal's raised eyebrow was his only acknowledgment of her attempt at humor. "At least you were using your head a little bit."

"A *little bit*!" Jessica's temper surged again. "You're a fine one to talk, I must say. You stand there asking me questions while I'm supposed to ignore what *you* were doing out there. Aside from—"

"—scaring you to death," he put in dryly. "We've been over that part of the script already."

"Yes, well . . . I can linger on it if I want to."

"You must be getting back to normal."

"That doesn't sound like a compliment," she retorted with a defiant gaze.

He held up his hands in mock surrender and then said, "Damn!" as water from the washcloth he was holding dripped down his arm. "Now, look," he said, tossing the cloth in the bathroom and then coming back to stand on the threshold again, "we have the rest of the night to snipe at each other, but I intend to find out first if you're up to it physically. I'll get your jacket and then we'll see how you do walking to the car."

"I'll be damned! You haven't paid one bit of attention to what I've been saying."

"That's where you're wrong. I could repeat it word for word—just the way you've been doing. Now, will you stop complaining and tell me what jacket you want?"

"No." Jessica crossed her arms over her breast defiantly. "I'm not moving an inch until you come up with some answers."

He sighed and rubbed the back of his neck. "Make

it one answer and take a rain check on the rest until after you've seen the doctor."

"Well . . ."

As she hesitated, he added, "You don't really have a choice. I'm just humoring you because the neighbors would probably talk if I hauled you out of here kicking and screaming."

"I'd like to see you try," she announced with fire in her eyes.

"Well, I wouldn't."

His resigned tone made Jessica give him another look. There was a grayish tinge to his skin that showed he still wasn't in mint condition after his experiences of the night before, and she felt instant remorse.

"All right, I'll behave," she told him, swinging her feet over the side of the bed. "But only if you let the doctor take another look at you tonight too."

A slanted smile softened his expression momentarily. "One look at the two of us and he'll probably put us on a retainer fee. Do you feel up to walking?"

The last came as she got to her feet but stayed against the bed to make sure that a vertical position was possible. Aside from a brief woozy interval at the outset, she decided that she was going to live. "I'm fine," she announced. "I honestly don't see any need for all this."

"I'm having you checked out," Cal announced, cutting into her words firmly. "And now, about that jacket or sweater or whatever."

"There's one on a hook just inside that door," she told him, nodding toward the other bedroom.

"Okay, stay there and I'll get it." He was back in a moment carrying a windbreaker over his arm. After she shrugged into it, he gestured toward the front door.

"Hang on a minute, Mr. Sloane," she said, staying stubbornly where she was. "You didn't give me an answer."

"You didn't ask the question."

"Honestly—" She broke off and took a deep breath to lower her voice. "All right. Exactly what kind of surveillance were you doing out there?"

"I was checking for signs of illegal activity."

"But from whom? And where?"

"That's more than one question," he said, giving her a gentle but definite shove on the derriere to steer her toward the front door. Then, feeling her resistance, he relented to say, "Okay, so it was Bruce's boat and I was curious about that noise aboard too."

She turned to face him as he opened the door. "You can't leave it like that. It's like opening a can of worms and then just walking away."

"I'll try to put them back *after* the doctor checks you out. Now, stop complaining and hang on to me. I'd just as soon that you didn't take another header into the shrubbery tonight. I might not survive it."

Jessica gave a nervous giggle and then fell silent as they moved out into the quiet of the night. Her glance honed in immediately on the moorage where Bruce Lightner's big sailboat bobbed in the water.

"Nothing happening there," Cal said, showing that his attention was on the same thing. "There's just enough current to cause that motion. See . . ." He gestured ahead of them as they moved toward the stairs. "It's happening all along the marina." His grip tightened on her elbow as they made their way down to the path. "Are you okay? I could carry you."

"You'll have to practice saying that more enthusiastically," she chided.

His shoulders shook as he chuckled. "Notice that I

didn't say how far I could carry you. You'd be safe for the first fifty feet or so. Maybe further if you really can't hack it."

"I'm okay," she assured him, and decided that she truly meant it. "In fact, I feel an awful fool even heading for a doctor."

"Forget it. You haven't been given a choice."

Cal sounded as if his attention really wasn't on their conversation, and Jessica noticed that he was paying an inordinate amount of attention to the things around them. "Are you looking for something special?" she asked finally as they neared the parking lot.

"Huh?" This time, there was no hiding the fact that his thoughts had been elsewhere. "I'm sorry," he said, sounding as if it were an effort to make conversation. "What did you say?"

Jessica gave a nervous glance over her own shoulder. "It doesn't matter for now. Where are you parked?"

"Here on the end," he said, holding the gate that separated the condo landscaping from the asphalt parking area. "Hang on a second and I'll unlock the car door."

Jessica slipped gratefully into the front seat but didn't completely relax until he'd gotten behind the wheel and she heard the automatic door lock. After that, she waited until he'd started up through the now-deserted ferry-landing area before she said, "Okay, now maybe you'll tell me why you're so intrigued with Bruce Lightner's boat. And don't try to evade the issue, because you were watching it earlier today too. When we were having lunch and you . . . er . . . grabbed me."

"I'd better work on my technique," he said, sounding amused. "Grabbed? It couldn't have been that bad. How about 'approached enthusiastically'?"

"I'm sticking by 'grabbed.' And now, let's get back to my question."

"There is a certain decided resemblance between you and a wire-haired terrier that I know. He doesn't give up either."

"I happen to like wire-haired terriers," she informed him loftily. "And I will continue to dig in your backyard until I find out what particular bone you're hiding. Do I make myself clear?"

"Oh, yes. Loud and clear. Okay, for what it's worth—there is a general opinion that Mr. Lightner is engaged in several undertakings besides real estate in this part of the world. Also that he conducts a great deal of his business beyond the coastal limits, or inside the coastal limits if it suits his convenience."

"I see. And tonight?"

"We received a tip that he was scheduled for another rendezvous—destination unknown. Maybe he's just planning a late date."

Jessica ignored that and shifted in the seat to survey him. "How do you know all this?"

"I just said I'd answer a question or two—not provide you with a legal brief." He shot her a sideways glance before giving his attention to the turnoff as they approached the hospital at the outskirts of town. "You'll have to take the rest on faith until the situation is resolved. I'm sorry that you got involved, but . . ."

From his intonation, it was clear that he still thought most of her troubles were of her own making. It became an established fact when he added pointedly, "If you'll just stay out of the way for a day or two, everything should be okay. As a matter of fact, I'd strongly advise a nice long weekend in Seattle. You could go shopping or sightseeing while you're there."

"Or climb Mt. Rainier if I had a free afternoon." Her sarcasm was withering. "You sound just like a tour guide. Well, I'm not leaving the island, so you can scratch that idea."

He mumbled something in response that didn't bear translating, and she didn't try—content to get quickly out of the car after he'd braked at the emergency entrance of the hospital.

"You don't have to come in," she told him when she heard the slam of his door and footsteps on the concrete behind her.

"It's the least I can do, since I'm the one responsible for your being here."

"Well, it really isn't necessary," she announced as he opened the glass doors to the emergency section and gestured her into the well-lit foyer.

"If nothing else, I have to protect my reputation," he said, giving her a wry glance. "The mood you're in, I could find myself behind bars."

"Relax—it's hardly a 'battered-woman' syndrome," she told him scathingly, and then fell silent as she noticed the wide-eyed emergency receptionist listening behind the counter.

Cal took over, handling the details smoothly, and Jessica found herself content to let him. It was difficult to act as a role model of modern womanhood when her knees were still apt to go rubbery at the odd moment.

Fortunately, she was the only patient in the section just then, and she was swiftly ushered into a clean cubicle and told to sit on an examination table. Cal hovered watchfully until the doctor appeared.

"I didn't expect to see you again so soon," the man

commented to Cal, and then frowned as he turned to Jessica. "You two seem to be having an almighty run of bad luck."

She managed a smile. "Not really. Frankly I didn't think this visit was necessary, but—"

"I did," Cal cut in. "I was so impressed with your service last night, I thought it bore repeating. I'll be waiting outside," he told Jessica, and gave the doctor a brief nod.

"Hey, wait a minute," the latter said before he could close the curtain behind him. "How are *you* feeling? How's your head?"

"Just as hard as ever, thanks. Miss Webster will testify to that," Cal replied, and went on out into the hall.

"He's a pretty determined guy," the doctor said mildly, turning to Jessica and pulling a stethoscope out of his pocket.

"Isn't he?" she concurred, managing a brilliant smile that didn't reach her eyes.

"Friend of yours?"

"You could say that."

There was a decided pause, and then, aware that he wasn't going to get anywhere with that topic, the doctor cleared his throat and switched to safer medical grounds.

The examination didn't take long and he looked puzzled as he finally straightened. "Frankly I can't find any physical reason why you should have a fainting episode like this one tonight. You say that there isn't any dizziness now?"

"Not a bit." Jessica hadn't volunteered the information about Cal's part in her malady and didn't intend to. "I feel fine, thanks."

"Well, I can't dispute your word," the doctor said,

sounding as if he'd like to. "However, I strongly suggest that you have your own doctor run the rule over you once you get home. I don't like these 'out-of-the-blue' happenings but I can't find an answer for this one."

"Thank you for all your trouble," Jessica said, sliding off the table onto the floor of the emergency-room cubicle and looking around for her purse.

"I'd also suggest that you go home and get into bed, no matter what else Mr. Sloane might have in mind," the doctor said, putting his stethoscope back in his pocket.

"Oh, he won't object to that prescription," Jessica assured him, and then felt the color run into her face as the doctor's eyebrows climbed. "He's just a friend of my family's," she finished weakly.

"In that case, I've made another wrong diagnosis," the doctor said with a skeptical look. "Do you think you'll have any trouble sleeping tonight? I can prescribe a sedative if you want one."

"No, thanks, I'm just fine." The words were out before Jessica became aware that she was repeating herself. Suddenly a quick exit seemed like the best solution. "I'll take care of my bill at the business office right away."

"There's no hurry," he replied, twitching back the curtain and ushering her ahead of him toward the reception room. "I want to take another look at Mr. Sloane's head and see if he's doing as well as he claims."

Jessica was amused to see that Cal wasn't charmed about undergoing even a brief reexam, but other than being downright rude, he couldn't avoid it.

She interrupted his protests to say, "I'm going to settle my account. I'll be waiting in the reception room."

He was more successful in his arguments than she'd anticipated, because by the time she'd finished writing a check and getting her insurance claim, he came up behind her.

"Ready?" he asked when she turned from the counter.

"Yes—but what about you?"

"I took care of the charges on that other visit," he said briefly. "Let's get going."

They were out in the parking lot and getting in the car again before he added, "The doctor said you were going to be fine."

"I am fine. Right now," Jessica told him. "I felt like a fool to be wasting his time." She slammed the door behind her for emphasis and waited for him to get behind the wheel before it occurred to her that she'd been less than gracious about the whole inter-lude. "I'm sorry," she began hesitantly when he'd switched on the ignition and was backing carefully out of their parking space. "I know you meant well, and there's no reason for me to take your head off. Especially when you can't be feeling great after last night either."

His sigh was audible even over the sound of the engine. "That's okay. Maybe we should declare a truce to get us through the rest of the night. I promise I won't hold you to it once you're back to full strength."

Jessica half-turned in the seat and saw that a crooked smile had softened his normally stern expression. She was deciding that it made him look years younger even as she said, "That sounds fair enough."

"Good." His tone became brisk again. "Then you won't object if I take you back to the apartment so you can go straight to bed."

Her eyes narrowed at that ultimatum. "By myself?"

"That was what I had in mind. Why? Does that upset your social schedule?"

"Don't be silly. I just thought that maybe you—" Suddenly she became aware of what she was saying and stopped abruptly.

"That's generous of you," Cal said, not bothering to hide his amusement. "And I must say it's the best invitation I've had tonight."

"Cut it out!" she snapped. "You know what I meant."

"Well, there's always hope. Hey, stop that!" he said, fending off the blow she'd aimed at his shoulder. "You'll have us back in the accident ward."

"Then don't make bad jokes."

"You don't do much for a man's ego."

"That isn't one of your problems, as we both know. If you want this peace pact to hold—"

"—I'd better change the subject," he finished with resignation. "Okay. Thanks for the invitation, though."

"It was *not* an invitation."

"But I'll have to decline," he continued, ignoring her interruption. "At least this time. If you're giving out rain checks, I promise to be at the head of the line."

She shook her head in mock dismay. "That doctor obviously should have kept you under wraps a little longer."

"Tell him that the next time you see him." Cal braked at the intersection of Main Street and turned left on it. "I'll walk you back to the apartment and see that you lock the door behind you."

"What are you going to do?" Jessica asked, forgetting to be diplomatic.

"There are a couple of people I have to see later tonight."

"You mean Bruce Lightner and his friend."

"Of course not. If I'd planned a meeting with him, I wouldn't have been hanging around in the shrubbery with you."

"You do have a gift with words," she said in saccharine tones. "It's a wonder that you haven't been laid out in lavender on a deserted beach before this."

"I'm surprised myself." He slowed as they reached the end of the condo parking lot, letting the car coast down toward the water, and then pulled gently to a stop. When Jessica reached for the door handle, he put a hand on her arm to stop her. "One more thing. If your plans for the future happen to include a young man named Judd Harley—I suggest you change them."

Jessica was so surprised at his ultimatum that her mouth fell open. Then her lips came together and she said coldly, "Exactly what do you know about Judd Harley?"

"He's a hired help of Bruce's and he's tried his luck with every available female on the island at one time or another. That's about all."

"But you know I spent part of the day with him?"

He nodded calmly, not the least impressed with her austere manner. "So I heard."

"While you were larking around with another notorious 'local.' I suppose that's perfectly okay."

"If you're talking about Valerie," he said, annoyed, "you know damned well I did."

She shook off his hand and reached for the door handle again. "And did you give her a lecture about going to the movies with Judd?"

His eyebrows drew together in an ominous line. "Tonight?"

"That's right," she said as she got out of the car.

"Your sources must be a little behind the ticker. Is there anything else you'd like to know?"

"Not now." He stepped out of the car on his side and slammed the door before meeting her in front of the hood. "I can think of several things I'd like to do, though."

"I can't imagine what you mean." As he caught her elbow in a tight grip and steered her toward the path, she tried to shake him off. "I am perfectly capable of finding my way to the apartment alone."

"I want to know for sure that you're behind a locked door for the rest of the night. Are you sure that doctor said you were all right?"

"Of course—I'm perfectly fine, but I'm getting a little bored. You've been harping on the same subject for the last five minutes. 'Go directly to the apartment,' 'Lock the door,' 'Don't stop on the way,' 'Don't try to collect two hundred dollars,' 'Don't—' "

"I get the idea," he said, opening the gate behind the building.

"I admit that you have a point," she said then, beginning to regret that she'd lost her temper again.

He drew an imaginary star in the air with a lean forefinger. "Praises be! The woman admits that there's method in my madness. I didn't think the day would ever come." As they passed a dim light illuminating the path, he stooped to see the face of his watch. "Damn! I've got to check in."

"Go ahead." Jessica decided the least she could do was make his task a little easier. "We're practically on the front doorstep now and you don't have to tuck me in, for heaven's sake."

"I don't know about that." Cal pulled up, but there was a worried frown on his face as he stared at her. "It's just that so many things have gone wrong . . ."

He switched in mid-sentence as another thought occurred to him. "And you'll give Judd Harley a wide berth?"

A chuckle escaped her lips. "You don't have to worry about that. He'd probably go across the street to avoid me. I managed an imaginary case of hiccups all the way from English Camp to Friday Harbor and it didn't do much for his libido."

Cal laughed. "It seems I'm giving advice to an expert."

"Not really." She sobered as she asked, "Do you have any solid evidence against him?"

He shook his head. "Henry just came through with that snippet of information from his hospital bed. Now that he's had time to think things over, he's decided to be a little more cooperative."

"But Henry was a victim. . . ."

"That's right. But some people are wondering how and why he was involved in the first place." Cal shot another glance at his watch. "There isn't time to discuss it now."

"I know, you have to go," Jessica said, resigned. "Maybe the next time we get together, you'll have some answers to go with the questions."

"I sure as hell hope so." He gave her another push down the path, but this time his touch was considerably more gentle. In fact, it seemed to Jessica as if his fingers were reluctant to leave her shoulders. "I'll watch you to the end of the building," he said when she looked back after a few steps. "Get a move on."

"You're going to turn my head with compliments like that," she said, lingering a moment longer. "Maybe you should look for another instructor on how to handle women. Torquemada isn't on the suggested reading list these days."

"Now she tells me." He shook his head in mock resignation. "I'll have to check out another library book. In the meantime, would you kindly—please—get the hell on down the path."

Jessica smiled and did as he asked. She waved to him as she reached the last building, where the walk turned toward the water. It was a temptation to watch him all the way back to the parking-lot gate, but she kept faithfully on her way.

The least she could do was follow instructions for a change, because, shaky though their peace was, it was showing definite possibilities. Once all the furor on the island was resolved, they might even be able to wipe the slate clean and start again. It was ridiculous how much enjoyment she had sparring with him. And just once in a while, when she caught a glimpse of his slanted grin, she had the feeling that he felt exactly the same way. Of course, that was no guarantee that it would lead to something more permanent.

From the way she'd seen him behave in Valerie's company, it was evident that he didn't need assistance in dealing with the feminine sex. It was more likely that he'd need help in pushing them away.

Jessica was so intent on that unhappy realization that when a figure emerged from the shadow on the condo's front porch, she almost fainted away again. "Good God!" she said, drawing in her breath sharply as she grabbed the porch railing to steady herself.

"Sweetie, I *am* sorry," Valerie Long said, giving her a concerned look. "I've been standing here knocking on your front door, but I certainly didn't mean to scare you to death. You're all right, aren't you?" The last came as Jessica still clung to the railing.

By then her momentary dizziness had subsided

and Jessica was able to nod. "I'm okay, thanks. I was thinking of something else—that's all. Just a second and I'll get the door unlocked." A sudden idea struck her as she inserted the key, and she looked over her shoulder. "Are you alone?"

Valerie's eyebrows climbed in surprise. "Of course. Why? Were you expecting someone else?"

Jessica almost said, "I thought maybe you had Judd parked nearby," but managed a diplomatic, "Not at all," before she pushed the door wide and switched on the light in the foyer. "Please come in."

"I really didn't come calling." Valerie spread her hands wide in a disarming gesture. "Henry phoned me—he wanted me to give you some of the papers on his project at the Institute. He needs them right away."

A frown creased Jessica's forehead. "But he's still in the hospital. I don't understand. What things? And where are they?"

Valerie shook her head. "I'm such a scatterbrain. They're in his office in the Institute. I thought if you came and got them tonight that you could send them down to him on the morning plane. Or maybe take them in person. Cal said something about your spending a few days in Seattle."

"He must have gotten his dates mixed," Jessica informed her firmly. "I have no intention of leaving the island right now. If Henry needs the stuff, I suppose I could ship it down to him, but I'm wondering . . ."

As her voice dropped, Valerie cut in quickly, "Wondering what?"

"Well . . ." Jessica raised her palms in an apologetic gesture. "To be honest—why me?" She went on quickly, "I mean, he certainly is a friend of the family, but when it comes to his work, I would think he'd want one of you to handle things."

Valerie's chin went up an inch. "Frankly, I would have thought so too, but Henry is acting very strangely these days. It didn't seem right to argue with a man in the hospital, though, so I just humored him and said you'd take care of it." She gave Jessica an appealing look. "Was that all right?"

"Well, I guess so."

"Good." Valerie reached for the doorknob almost before Jessica uttered her hesitant agreement. "I hope you can come along now, because I have plans for later on. Where are you going now?"

Valerie's annoyed question caught Jessica when she'd just taken a few steps down the hall toward her bedroom. "To get a heavier coat." It was an effort for Jessica to keep her tone pleasant in view of the way Valerie seemed determined to run things. "Is there something wrong with that idea?"

The other woman gave a trill of laughter. "Of course not—but I don't think you'll need one. That windbreaker you're wearing will be all you need in the car, and I am awfully late." She pulled the door open suggestively. "Okay?"

"I guess so." Jessica hovered an instant longer in the hallway as she decided she didn't really have a valid objection. She started back to the door, oddly reluctant to leave the condo, which seemed even more inviting than usual. The warm perfumed air of the interior made her realize how much she'd been looking forward to settling down on the couch and staring at a cozy fire in the fireplace. There was even the forlorn hope that Cal might check in a little later to report on his success. She thought for an instant of leaving him a brief note and then decided against it after seeing Valerie shoot another glance at the watch on her wrist. It was probably silly to even think of such a thing, since the Institute was a bare ten minutes' drive through town, beyond the public marina on the far shore.

"Ready?" Valerie wasn't tapping her foot but she wasn't making any attempt to hide her impatience either.

"Okay." Jessica checked her purse and followed her out onto the porch, taking care to lock the door behind them before following her down the darkened steps.

At the end of the building, Valerie surprised her by turning left toward the hillside instead of following the main path toward the parking lot.

"Where are you headed?"

Valerie slackened her pace slightly a she glanced back. "This is a shortcut to the parking lot up beside the street. Where the general public is expected to stay," she added, sarcasm underlining her words. "All those spaces where you've been leaving the car are for condo residents—or didn't you read the signs?"

"I guess I didn't pay any attention."

"Well, this is really closer," Valerie admitted, heading for a steep set of stairs, "and I keep telling myself that it's good for my waistline. You can manage, can't you?"

The doctor in the emergency room wouldn't have approved of such shenanigans, Jessica told herself wryly when she reached the first landing and turned toward the final flight that climbed the steep hill.

"You really should get in better shape," Valerie said when Jessica reached the top landing beside her.

Jessica clung to the railing, trying not to reveal how the climb had exhausted her. It was a tempta-

tion to say that there were extenuating circumstances—
that normally she'd give her a run for her money, or
at least a short climb—but she merely nodded.
Damned if she'd start volunteering information about
the night's activities!

"If you're ready . . ." Valerie tossed the words
over her shoulder as she unlocked the door of her car,
parked just a few feet away.

"I see what you mean about this being a shortcut,"
Jessica said, trying to maintain a pleasant atmosphere
as she got in and Valerie slid into the driver's seat
beside her. "It's awfully dark up here, though. I
wonder what the town council has against streetlights?"

"They cost money." Vallerie switched on the ignition and stopped to put on her seat belt before backing out onto the deserted street. "Besides, there's
nothing to be afraid of in this part of the world.
That's why people live in small towns. We don't
have to worry about street gangs and vandalism—
things that I suppose you face every day."

Jessica smothered a laugh. It had been far from a
quiet weekend since she'd arrived. Much more country life and she'd be a prime candidate for a barred
room and a thick white jacket that fastened in the
back. "It's certainly different from life in the fast
lane," she admitted noncommittally, "although I don't
move in jet-set circles in Texas. More the usual 'get
up, go to work, and go home again' routine."

"That isn't what Cal seems to think," Valerie said,
shooting her a sideways glance. She braked as they
came down the hill, looked carelessly both ways along
a quiet thoroughfare, and accelerated again. "I don't
know why I even bothered to slow down. Once the
movie's over, this town is completely deserted. Everybody lives for Saturday night, when sometimes

people stay up until midnight. God! It's like being stuck in the eighteenth century."

"Then why do you stay?"

"Because the salary's good and Henry is easy to work for." Valerie's tone was almost defiant. "But if he doesn't come back, I don't know what will happen."

"You mean, you'd have to change bosses at the Institute?"

Valerie gave a snort of laughter. "It's a nice thought. Frankly, I don't have much faith in it."

"Why is that?"

"Because I haven't been too cooperative with some of the administrators and they'd love to have an excuse to send me a pink slip. If Henry isn't around to defend me . . ." she shrugged and then accelerated almost recklessly along the deserted highway, as if that was the easiest way to ease her annoyance.

Jessica drew in her breath as they swerved back on their side of the two-lane road when a car came around a sharp curve toward them.

"Idiot!" Valerie muttered, and then braked abruptly to turn off on the gravel lane leading the mile or so down to the Institute.

Jessica hoped she was referring to the other driver and sighed in relief that they were off the main road. Considering the way most people drove, they really didn't need any more excitement on the island, she decided. Valerie must have taken beginning lessons from Judd, but hadn't bothered to complete the course.

"You're awfully quiet all of a sudden," the secretary said as they bounced and jounced their way down the track, which was full of potholes.

It probably wouldn't be diplomatic to mention that she'd missed hitting a couple of them, Jessica thought, and wondered if she'd get an honest-to-goodness set of hiccups from swallowing all her traitorous thoughts.

"I hope my driving doesn't make you nervous," Valerie went on airily as they plowed through another pothole that threatened the future of the car's suspension. "You don't have to worry—I have an excellent record."

"I'm sure you have," Jessica murmured politely. It wasn't surprising, since the natives probably took to the shoulder as soon as they recognized her car.

Just then they turned off the track to the curving drive of the Institute and Jessica got her first glance at the building through the trees. "It looks awfully dark." Her hesitant words were out before she realized, and brought a trill of laughter from the woman at her side.

"You don't honestly think they'd leave a candle in the window for us, do you?" Valerie replied, pulling up with a flourish in front of the building and turning off the ignition.

"Of course not." Jessica opened her car door and stepped out onto the path. She peered down toward the building, barely able to make out the entrance through the gloom. "These trees even cut off the moonlight—I think we should have brought a flashlight."

Valerie got out on her side and shut the door with a bang. "Stop worrying," she admonished, coming around to Jessica's side to catch her forearm in a surprisingly strong grip. "I can find my way around this place blindfolded," she said, walking them down the path. "We've all practically had to, since the first thing they do when they trim the budget is cut off the outdoor lighting. Personally I think that kind of penny-pinching is absurd, but nobody listens to me."

She made no attempt to hide the bitterness in her
tone, and Jessica's eyebrows climbed. It was a good
thing that Henry's secretary had some outstanding
physical assets, because she certainly wasn't a happy
person to be around. But then, there was no telling
how she behaved when her companion was a good-
looking, available man. No telling, Jessica decided,
but she had a darned good idea.

She had to give the woman her due, though, because they pulled up at the darkened front entrance
of the building shortly afterward without a misstep
on the way down. Valerie had her key ready to open
the heavy door. She gestured Jessica into the foyer an
instant later and shut the door behind them—throwing
a deadbolt home with an audible click.

"What . . . why—?"

"Security," Valerie said, cutting into Jessica's protest. "I'd lose my head if I were responsible for a
break-in by coming after hours."

Jessica stood in the dim foyer, trying to get her
eyes accustomed to the gloom. "Well, would you
please turn on some light now? They certainly can't
have your head for that. If anybody objects, I'll put a
quarter in a contributions box toward the operating
fund." She glanced around them. "They must have a
contributions box here somewhere—I've never seen
any kind of institute that didn't."

"I guess there's one on the counter," Valerie murmured distractedly.

Jessica stared at her, surprised to hear her sounding ill-at-ease. Surely she couldn't be seriously worried about coming onto her working premises after
hours. As she watched the secretary search through
her purse, she asked, "Is there anything wrong?"

Valerie gave a start, almost dropping her purse in

the process. "Of course not," she said defiantly. "What makes you think something's wrong?"

Jessica shrugged. "I just wondered why we're still standing up here in the foyer."

"Mainly because I'm looking for the key to the file cabinet where Henry keeps the notes from his special projects. But now I've found it"—she waved the key triumphantly aloft—"so we might as well go on down."

"Down?"

Valerie stopped on her way to a nearby stairway leading to the lower floor. "Do you have to keep repeating what I say? You sound like a parrot." She started toward the dimly lit staircase again, adding over her shoulder, "There's a perfectly good reason for going down. That's where Henry's office is. If that's all right with you."

Valerie's sarcasm brought out an unladylike urge in Jessica that wavered between giving the woman a good shove or heading straight back to the front door—leaving Henry and his secretary to sort out their problems in their own fashion. Then Jessica remembered that she was dependent on Valerie for the trip back to town and had to forgo the luxury of such actions. Instead she followed her silently, thinking that at least the poor light hid her annoyance, which was probably a good thing. She'd been an idiot to take pity on the two of them in the first place.

Jessica's foot slipped off the curving stair-step as she neared the bottom and she gave silent thanks that she'd been hanging on to the banister. Valerie had already reached the lower floor, flicking on one small bulb before striding down the empty hallway, which had closed doors on either side. Jessica screwed up her eyes to peer at some of the nameplates and discovered that most of the Institute's lab work was done on the lower premises.

A sudden quiet descended when Valerie stopped in front of a door at the end of the hallway and opened it. She reached inside to flip on the office light, and then it went off again.

"Hey, wait a minute," Jessica said, moving down the hall to join her. "Don't tell me we're going to have to search by candlelight?" When there was no response, she hesitated, still in the middle of the darkened hallway. "Valerie?"

"For heaven's sake," came a prompt response. "What are you waiting for?"

"Well, nothing, I guess," Jessica said, walking slowly toward the doorway. "What happened? Did the light burn out?"

"I suppose so." Valerie's tone was careless. "It's all right. I have a flashlight in my purse, and there's a light on Henry's desk—once I get over to it."

Jessica drew a relieved breath as she reached the doorway and peered into the darkened interior. "Is there anything I can do to help?"

"Well, you might try that switch by the door again," Valerie replied from the other side of the room.

"Okay." Jessica fumbled on the wall beside her. "But if it didn't work before, I don't think I'll have any luck this . . . Good Lord! I'll be—" The sudden light of the overhead fixture had brought a triumphant spurt of enthusiasm to her voice, which broke off abruptly as she viewed the masculine figure standing alongside Valerie by a desk at the far side of the room.

"You're not any more surprised than I am," Bruce Lightner said, sounding decidedly disagreeable. He turned to Valerie, who was clutching the strap of her shoulder bag with nervous fingers. "I suppose you have a good reason for bringing Miss Webster along."

"She told me that Henry wanted some papers sent down to him in the hospital," Jessica put in when Valerie didn't immediately respond.

"Ah, yes—Henry," Bruce Lightner said.

It wasn't what he said but the way he said it that made Jessica realize that something was definitely amiss. The man even looked different, clad in dark slacks and a black long-sleeved sweater that changed him from the robust, good-natured real-estate salesman to a suddenly ominous figure whose middle-aged face was far from genial as he stared at them.

"I'm still waiting for your explanation, Valerie," he said again, in a soft level voice that seemed all the more dangerous by its very restraint.

"She came back before I had a chance to get away." Valerie's tone was a mixture of defiance and pleading. "All I could do was stay on the porch and pretend that I'd just arrived."

"Just arrived?" Jessica frowned, trying to remember, and then she fixed Valerie with an accusing look. "You mean that the whole thing was a hoax? That you'd—"

"That she'd been through your apartment," Bruce said, sounding like a man who was bored by the whole discussion. He turned to Valerie and added grudgingly, "It sounds as if you did something right, at least."

She shrugged. "It was a lost cause. I didn't find anything. Cal must be covering his tracks better than we thought as far as *she* goes . . ." She shot a disparaging glance in Jessica's direction. "There's nothing to report. Maybe Cal was telling the truth about her."

"Not quite." Bruce kept his tone noncommittal. "He neglected to mention that it was Jessica's house at the beach—" He broke off to give her a mock bow that was anything but courteous, and then went on. "Fortunately I had already checked that out. What we don't know is how much Henry has told her. He's a man that has difficulty keeping his mouth shut."

From his manner, Lightner might have been telling about the daily activity on the stock market, and Jessica found her resentment growing. "I'm here, you know," she announced to both of them. "And I do speak English and understand words of more than one syllable."

"Oh, I don't doubt that," Bruce said, fixing his attention directly on her for a change. "That's the trouble. At least part of the trouble. The main part—as you said—is that you are here." He looked down at his nails on one pudgy hand and absently buffed them against his sweater sleeve. Then he raised his glance again and said levelly to her, "It would have been much better for you if you'd been anywhere else." He held up his palm as she opened her mouth to object. "The fact that you didn't plan to come— that it wasn't your idea—doesn't make any difference. Not a particle of difference, my dear Jessica." His sudden smile was a grimace. "That's the way of things, isn't it? Now I'm afraid you've cast your lot with us—at least for the moment."

"You mean we'll take her along?" Valerie was aghast.

Bruce's smile erased as if by magic. "Maybe you have a better idea. After all, you're the one who made the mistake of bringing her here."

She shrank visibly under his look. "I'm sorry, Bruce. I didn't know what else to do."

Jessica tried to ignore the lump of fear in her throat

that had suddenly made it difficult to swallow. "There's quite a simple solution. Just take me back to town. I'll overlook Valerie's botched housebreaking attempt. Actually I should have known she'd been through the place," she continued. "Your perfume," she told Valerie. "I remember now—the fragrance was in the front hall when we went in." Her eyes narrowed as another memory surfaced. "It was in the apartment upstairs the other night, too—when I found the place ransacked." Then, as she saw Bruce's jaw harden, she gave herself a mental jab. If she kept on with her accusations, she was practically asking for a one-way trip to the unknown. From the look on his face, it might already be too late to cover her mistakes.

His next words confirmed it. "I'm afraid that's why we'll have to take you with us, Jessica. At least for part of the trip." He gave her a flashing salesman's smile that was a travesty of the real thing. "You don't mind if I call you Jessica, do you?"

Jessica almost came back with, "I'd rather you called me a cab," and then shook her head at such inanities. That dive she'd taken into the shrubbery in Cal's grasp must have had a greater effect on her mind than she'd realized.

Bruce apparently thought she was taking his question seriously, because his wolflike grin flashed again as he said, "It won't make any difference in the long run, my dear." He reached for an attaché case that was on the desk and tucked it carefully under his arm. "For now, let's all go aboard the boat."

"The boat?"

Valerie gave Jessica an annoyed look. "Bruce's boat. What did you think?"

"Well, if you're going back to the moorage by the

condo, it won't be any trouble to drop me off,"
Jessica told them.

Bruce moved toward the office door, shepherding
her in front of him. "That's the least of your problems or ours. Anyhow, you have things a little con-
fused. My boat isn't at the moorage. We're tied up at
the dock here—so much more convenient."

"It doesn't matter where you're tied up." Jessica's
voice rose in frustration. "You can't just hijack me.
What's Cal going to think? As soon as he finds out
that I'm not at the condo, he'll sound an alarm." Her
glance focused on Bruce's face. Instead of appearing
upset by her threat, he looked almost smug. "Maybe
I don't know what's going on—but he certainly does,"
she finished, trying to sound as if she believed it.

"He might have a few ideas, but not enough to
bother us." Bruce gestured her ahead of him again.
"And as for coming after you—I wouldn't pin many
hopes on it. We've taken care that he's following
another lead. One that's going to be a very dead
end." His heavy shoulders shook in amusement. "If
you'll forgive the expression."

"I don't care what expressions you use," Jessica
said, pulling up on the threshold. "I'm not getting on
your boat. You can't make me. I'll . . . I'll . . . I'll
scream the place down if you lay a finger on me."

"Scream away, my dear," Bruce drawled. "There
might be a few rabbits and squirrels to hear you, but
I doubt if they'll care. And as for laying a finger on
you—I never indulge in things like that." His voice
deepened in distaste, as if he'd stepped in the small
puddle that was leaking from a bucket of marine
specimens in the hallway just beyond the door. "Fortunately I can always hire people to take care of such
emergencies."

Jessica turned to look over her shoulder to see what Valerie was doing. She might not have much of a chance against Bruce Lightner's weight and strength, but Valerie . . .

Lightner chuckled again. "You're getting the wrong idea again, my dear. Valerie isn't the one I had in mind." He was looking over her shoulder down the darkened hallway and giving a brief nod.

Too late, Jessica heard sudden footsteps behind her and she whirled to see Judd Harley come out from an office down the hall. There was just enough light to identify his mocking expression as, without comment, he caught her arm and bent it painfully up behind her.

She gasped with pain and tried wildly to get out of his grip. The smirk on his face deepened at her frantic efforts, but suddenly, as if tired of the commotion, he gave her a sudden shove toward the concrete-block wall beside them.

There was an instant of excruciating pain as her forehead banged into it, and then, mercifully, darkness blotted out the rest.

She didn't hear Bruce Lightner's terse, "Get her on the boat—we've wasted enough time," nor did she feel the impact when Judd lifted her limp body over one shoulder and followed his employer out to the quiet, gloomy pier, leaving a subdued Valerie to bring up the rear.

7

Jessica's first reaction upon regaining consciousness should have been stark terror at finding herself alone on the floor of a darkened cabin that was undoubtedly afloat, if the constant motion could be believed. Instead, her first thought was that seasickness would be the final blow. And she'd already had enough blows, since her head was aching abysmally from hitting that wall at the Institute.

She put up a tentative hand and winced as she felt the lump. The moist, sticky skin on her forehead confirmed that she had been bleeding earlier as a result. "You're a mess, woman," she told herself, and had to fight to hold back tears.

She chewed hard on the edge of her lower lip, determined to avoid such abject surrender. The proper approach was to look for something positive. At least she was alone in the cabin—that was a blessing. She got to her feet with an effort, and then clinging to a padded bench cushion which was part of the galley, she edged toward the door to check and see if it were locked.

A careful rattle of the knob brought a growl from the other side, and Jessica's hand dropped down again.

Evidently Kai, the German shepherd, was on duty to make sure that there wasn't any unauthorized traffic belowdeck.

She sank down on the cushion again in despair. They needn't have bothered with a German shepherd, she thought; at the moment a Chihuahua would have done as well. Her head was throbbing and her knees had a mind of their own when she tried to stand. Which meant that all she could do was sit on the damned bench and wait for Bruce Lightner or one of his minions to come and reveal her fate.

Resting her head gingerly against the bulkhead behind her, she tried to think if there were any factors in her favor. Certainly not if Judd were the man in charge. Even that fleeting glance of him in the Institute hallway before she lost consciousness showed that he was a man enjoying his work. He'd take a perverse delight in making her pay for that afternoon ride when she'd strung him along. Jessica moaned as she remembered, and dropped her face into her open palms, suddenly too weary and nauseated to cope.

The sailboat must be hitting some heavy swells, she thought, as the vessel rose and sank with sickening regularity—making her stomach react in the same way. She was too exhausted to try to find the head and decided grimly that the galley sink would have to serve. Judging her movement carefully, she slid down the bench and then lurched over to cling to the edge of the stainless-steel sink—waiting despairingly for the next bout of nausea to overtake her.

As she stood there, she was able to peer through the small porthole into the darkness outside. And it was dark, she confirmed, looking hopefully for any signs of marine traffic, since the possibility of trying to swim to shore wasn't realistic. The waters of the strait were icy year-round and survival time was almost on a par with the North Pacific. Of course there was always the chance that the sailboat was still close to land and not in the middle of the channel.

That thought cheered her momentarily, making her forget about her heaving stomach and throbbing head. A rattle in one of the galley lockers caught her attention an instant later, and she wondered if there might be something in the cupboard to help her defend herself later on. Certainly there was nothing in her purse that could qualify. She didn't even have a metal nail file. Frowning, she scanned the bench where she'd been sitting, and then the floor of the galley. Apparently Judd hadn't bothered to bring her purse along when he'd transported her to the boat. Or if he had, Bruce had appropriated it when they'd come aboard.

She gave a disdainful snort as she thought about him going through her belongings. At least he wouldn't find anything incriminating there.

Not that it would help her cause. Apparently she had committed the worst crime by just appearing on the scene at the Institute. Although it was hard to understand why he'd been so bothered. She doubted if he'd been rifling Henry's desk, and all that he'd taken from the room was that expensive-looking briefcase.

Jessica rubbed her forehead automatically, wincing when she touched the grazed skin and staring at her fingertips distastefully as she saw streaks of blood on them.

She moved back to the galley sink to put cold water on the bump, and then decided to settle for a towel to blot her skin. She looked around, finally pulling out a drawer under the sink. It was full of cutlery, and immediately she forgot all about the towel, staring instead at the array in front of her.

There was a paring knife that was possible. She tested the point against her thumb and then shook her head.

Whether it made sense or not, she couldn't stick a knife into any living thing, and there was no use thinking she could. So there must be something else, she thought, poking about in the drawer with a nervous finger. Or perhaps in the drawer next to it.

That yielded a potato masher and a good-size wooden mallet for tenderizing meat. Jessica drew a hopeful breath and then let it out again. The mallet looked good but there wasn't any place to hide it.

She was just about to close the drawer again when she came upon a small chrome mallet. Probably a bar utensil for crushing ice, she thought as she hefted it. It wasn't heavy enough to knock anybody out—or was it?

That was the trouble, she decided despairingly; she didn't know a damned thing about knocking people over the head. She tried to remember what she'd seen on the television cops-and-robbers shows. Maybe the idea was to just stun them—not try anything lethal.

The sound of voices beyond the door made her decide in a hurry that the mallet was better than nothing. She tucked it into her waistband and tried to pull her shirt over it, hoping that she could keep her arm at her side in case there was a suspicious bulge.

For an instant she debated feigning unconsciousness and then decided there wasn't anything to gain by it. They were obviously getting further from Friday Harbor and any possible help by the moment. If she waited too long, they'd be out of the strait altogether and into the frigid waters of the Pacific. Maybe they were already. Even as she explored that possibility, she discarded it. She couldn't have been out for the count that long—besides, while the swells were enough to make her queasy, they weren't enormous waves.

That realization gave her a little comfort, but not much, as the voices came closer. She recognized Bruce's authoritative tones as he said, "Take the dog and put him in the forward cabin—he'll only be a nuisance later on when our friends come aboard."

"You know I can't make him do anything I ask," Valerie objected, obviously disgruntled by her role.

Her words were reinforced by a sudden growl, and Jessica swallowed, wondering how she would have fared if she'd tried to venture into the hallway earlier.

"For God's sake, do I have to do everything myself?" Lightner complained. "Down, Kai. Come!"

Jessica heard the sound of retreating footsteps and, a moment later, another door slamming. She drew a hopeful breath, but it wasn't long before the footsteps came down the hall again.

"I don't know why you bother with that brute," Valerie said, annoyance still in her tone.

"Mainly because I trust him," Bruce snapped. "That's more than I can say for you and Judd."

"I keep telling you that this wasn't my fault. After she'd found me on the porch, I couldn't let her go in and discover that I'd been through the apartment. Lord knows what Cal would have made of that."

"There *were* alternatives. Unfortunately now there aren't any left." Bruce sounded thoroughly tired of the subject. "Get back up on deck and take over the wheel. Tell Judd that I want him to lower the dinghy. Don't stop to argue—just do it."

The last order came as he opened the door and pushed his way into the galley. His glance took in Jessica's defiant figure at the sink and he said, "Awake, are you? I thought you might be."

"No thanks to your friend Judd." She kept her tone level with an effort.

"Yes—well, he's inclined to be enthusiastic at times." Lightner might have been discussing the current price of potatoes for all the interest he displayed. He gave her another glance and then pulled the curtains over two narrow portholes on either side of the galley before switching on an overhead bulb. "That's better." He leaned his bulk against the stainless-steel refrigerator and appraised her like a piece of real estate. "You don't look as if you cared much for life afloat."

"I'm not keen on it."

"Of course, you realize that I could have disposed of you back at the Institute," he went on as if she hadn't spoken.

"Am I supposed to thank you for bringing me along?" Jessica's stomach muscles were knotted with tension but she was damned if she'd start cringing in front of the man. At least it would make a change, since Judd and Valerie certainly didn't talk back to him.

Her defiance must have struck a responsive chord, because for an instant he looked like the jovial real-estate operator she'd met on Main Street. "I'm afraid not," he replied, sounding as if he felt some sympathy for her. "Unfortunately, my dear, you were in the wrong place at the wrong time. In this game, the stakes are too high for any miscalculation. Our friend Henry found that out too, and paid the price. However, that has nothing to do with you. One thing at a time is my motto. I've always tried to keep my priorities right, and now you're at the top of the list."

The way he said it made Jessica shiver. "Exactly what does that mean?" she asked after a moment's silence.

"I don't want you along," he said flatly, and moved toward the door of the galley, "so we'll take another course of action. Judd should have the dinghy out by now."

Jessica ignored his gesture for her to precede him up the steps. His explanation was too glib—too fast. "You mean, Judd is going to put me ashore?" she asked.

"That's right." He motioned as the sound of the sailboat's motor throttled down. "He must be lowering the dinghy now. After you, my dear."

There was something in his expression that made Jessica linger an instant longer. Uncertainty and fear had her heart pounding, and the headache that she was trying to ignore echoed every stroke. As Bruce reached for her arm to enforce his order, she instinctively pulled away. There was a sudden muffled thud on the carpet at her feet and she could have groaned aloud. So much for her instrument of escape.

"Well, well—what have we here?" For a stocky man, Lightner moved fast as he retrieved the small hammer that had fallen from her waistband. He weighed it in his hand to say sarcastically, "Planning to crush ice for the cocktail hour? You should have asked me where I kept the gin." Reaching to an overhead locker, he pulled out a bottle and waved it in front of her nose. "Will this do? I'm a little short of vermouth, so you'll have to drink it straight." This time, there was no disguising his impatience as he shoved her toward the stairs. "Unfortunately there's no heat in the dinghy," he continued, keeping her in front of him as they reached the deck, "so maybe the gin will keep you warm."

It would take more than gin, Jessica realized as the chill wind which swept the dark waters of the strait cut through her clothes like a laser beam. She shivered and wrapped her arms around her to stare despairingly around them.

There was a shaded light at the stern where Valerie stood alongside the tiller. She had donned a dark windbreaker, and as Jessica watched, she straightened and shoved her hands in the pockets.

Bruce gave a snort of amusement at Jessica's worried look. "Judd's lashed the tiller. You don't think I'd leave anything to that featherbrain, do you?" As he turned to survey the deck, he released his grip on her. "I'm sure I don't have to worry about your taking a swim. Unless you're fond of long, cold ones."

An involuntary shudder went through her at his words. Even her first glance had shown that there wasn't another craft in sight, and the few scattered lights on the mainland were well over a mile away. The droplets of spray coming over the railing confirmed the icy temperature of the water. It would take a survival suit for her to even have a chance in it.

"You'll notice that we're just showing running lights now," Bruce said, apparently satisfied with what he'd seen on deck. "And we didn't have those until we were well away from shore, so if you're hoping for the cavalry to come over the hill—I wouldn't count on it. Now, it's time for you to get into the dinghy. Is everything ready, Judd?" he asked as the younger man made his way surefootedly from the bow toward them.

"Oh, yeah." As he approached, Jessica saw that he was carrying a small anchor at his side. "Ready to go for a ride, lady?" he asked, walking up beside her. "That bump on your head didn't bring back your hiccups, did it? Or maybe the cat's got your tongue," he drawled as Jessica just stared at him.

"We don't have any more time to waste," Lightner said. "Is the motor on the dinghy?"

"As ordered." Judd ducked his head to avoid the furled mainsail.

"Right. Then let's get on with it," Lightner said, catching Jessica's wrist in a tight grip.

She allowed herself to be towed behind him toward the stern. There wasn't really an alternative, she thought as she heard Judd's footsteps on her heels. Then that sound faded under the noise of the big sailboat's engine.

From the hooded light on the binnacle, she could just make out the trim dinghy bobbing in the boat's wake. It looked like the proverbial peapod as it bounced along, and the thought of sitting in it until they reached the shore made her stiff with terror.

"Pull it alongside, Judd, so Jessica won't get wet getting in," Lightner ordered, giving her a smile of mock solicitude.

"Sure thing," Judd said, putting the anchor down on the deck with a thud. He shortened the painter on the dinghy in one efficient gesture, showing that he wasn't a stranger to his duties aboard. At least he might be able to navigate properly to get them to shore, Jessica thought, trying to find something bearable about her situation.

As Lightner gestured for her to clamber over the

side into the frail dinghy, she cast one last desperate look around the dark waters—hoping that some craft might abruptly come into sight.

"I'm afraid it's going to be a lonely trip, my dear," Bruce said, raising his voice to be heard over the muted noise of the sailboat's motor. "That's the name of the game for sailors, though. Comfy?"

Jessica looked up at him as she clung to the middle seat of the dinghy, trying to ignore the inky currents cascading against the side.

"Incidentally, I've had to remove the underseat flotation foam," Bruce said as he helped Judd keep the small craft alongside. "I needed the space for storing some cargo on an earlier trip and I've just never gotten around to putting it back."

"This gets better and better," Jessica said, trying to keep her voice level through teeth that were almost chattering with cold and fear. "Are you sure that Judd knows how to run the motor?" She jerked her head toward the tiny outboard attached to the dinghy's stern.

There was a sudden trill of laughter and she glanced up to see that Valerie had abandoned the sailboat tiller to watch the goings-on. Bruce became aware of it at the same time and gestured abruptly to the other woman. "Get back and make sure that we're on course," he told her. "We're cutting the rendezvous time too fine for any mistakes, and our friends aren't the kind who'll wait around."

"I just wanted to see what was happening," Valerie complained, but she made her way back toward the lashed tiller.

"Oh, that reminds me." Bruce turned back along the deck and returned carrying the bottle of gin he had taunted her with earlier. "To help keep you

warm," he told Jessica, and passed it down into her
reluctant hands.

The thought of gin made her stomach heave even
more unpleasantly than the plunges that the dinghy
was taking. It was like being aboard a bucking bronco
but without the hope of a judge's whistle, Jessica
thought despairingly. She swallowed again and looked
up to Judd. "Hadn't you better come aboard and
start the motor to make sure it works?"

"Oh, it works," he replied, and grinned as he shot
a sideways glance at Lightner. "I made sure of that."

"What he means, my dear," Bruce said with a leer,
"is that it works when it's filled with gasoline. Right
now, there isn't any."

As his taunt sank in, Jessica's clutch on the seat
turned into a death grip. "You're crazy," she said
finally, barely able to get the words out of her tight
throat. "It's suicide to be in the middle of this strait
without power." She tried appealing to Judd. "Nobody in his right mind would try it."

"Oh, he agrees with you, so there's no need to
try and convince him," Bruce said, breaking into
her appeal. "But Judd isn't going along. I need him
here."

"You mean that I'm . . ." Her voice broke and
desperately she tried again. "You mean that I'll
be . . ."

". . . all alone. You've finally gotten the idea."
Lightner's voice was like a whiplash as he stared
down at her stricken face. "But I'll make sure you
won't go through any long, drawn-out suffering." As
he spoke, he stepped over to the metal anchor which
Judd had been carrying earlier and hoisted it aloft.
He carried it back to the rail, making sure that Jessica
couldn't miss the bare three feet of line attached to it.

"Since you don't have an engine, the least I can do is furnish an anchor."

Then, abruptly, before her horrified eyes, he threw the metal anchor down onto the side of the fiberglass craft, smiling with satisfaction as he saw one prong puncture the side of the boat at the waterline. At the same time, he gestured for Judd to release the rope tethering the dinghy.

Within seconds the big sailboat was beyond reach over the dark water. A terrified Jessica, crouching in the middle of the tiny bobbing dinghy, felt the icy waves surge into the bilge around her feet even as Bruce Lightner's mocking farewell floated through the nighttime air. "*Bon voyage*, my dear. Have a short trip and a merry one."

It was the last thing she heard before the dinghy settled into the valley of a mammoth swell and darkness settled like a shroud around her.

8

For an instant, terror kept Jessica crouching immobile like a wild thing. Her predicament was too cataclysmic for her exhausted mind to comprehend, and her first impulse was simply to collapse in the bottom of the dinghy and let the worst happen.

Fortunately the knowledge that the bilge water was getting deeper on her ankles reactivated her sense of self-preservation. Instinctively her hands went out to try to stem the flow that came through the hole each time the dinghy settled into a swell.

She watched the rivulets stream through her fingers and realized immediately that the "finger-in-the-dike" theory wasn't going to work. Each gush or trickle raised that ominous level in the bottom of the dinghy, so it was only a matter of time.

She stared almost blindly at the hole, willing herself to think rationally. The water was coming in—that meant that any kind of patch or plug should be on the outside. Chewing her lip so hard that it bled, she turned and searched the interior of the dinghy in the half-light. Unconsciously she gave thanks that there was enough moonlight coming through the thin cloud cover just then to enable her to see the outlines of her prison. Her eyes lit on the bottle of gin, rolling in the bilge by the bow, and she burst into hysterical laughter. Apparently there were two more options than she'd considered: she could consume the contents and pass out so that she'd never know her fate, or hit herself over the head with the bottle hard enough to accomplish the same thing.

It was the taste of blood in her mouth that brought her back to reality. At least she was wearing a skirt that might serve as a temporary plug in the hole, she decided, thinking fast as the dinghy plunged to the bottom of another swell.

She didn't dare risk standing up in the frail craft, so she took her skirt off in a kneeling position, finding it difficult to even slide the zipper with hands that felt like frozen fish fingers.

The fabric was already saturated by the time she slithered out of it. She started to wring out the part that had trailed into the bilge and then exclaimed in disgust. What in the devil was she worrying about! It would be soaked in two seconds anyway.

Trying to plug the hole from the outside wasn't easy. She inched forward on her stomach, managing to stay in the center of the dinghy as much as possible until she worked the upper part of her body carefully over the side. The salt water felt as if it had just come from the Antarctic as she fumblingly tried to stuff the material into the rough-edged hole.

She groaned aloud as the fabric almost sank on her first attempt, and she caught it by the hemline just before it disappeared. "Dear God," she prayed aloud, unaware that she'd even spoken as she tugged and pushed, finally managing to thread the material through the hole. She swore as it caught on the rough edges of the fiberglass and scraped her knuckles painfully in the process. But finally she achieved a stopgap of sorts and the gushing of water turned to an ominous seeping—but it was a start. She could buy extra time, she told herself desperately, if she could only find something to bail out the pool of water now surging around her ankles in the bilge.

Her glance went around the dinghy again, and she could have wept at the result. There wasn't time to try to take the motor apart—even supposing she had a screwdriver so she could use the metal housing as a bailer when she'd stripped it off. The narrow-necked gin bottle was totally useless unless . . . Her jaw clenched as she tried to determine whether she could smash the neck off the bottle so that she could use the bottom for a container. She hefted it experimentally and looked around before discarding it again. The way her luck was running, she'd either cut her wrists in the attempt or knock another hole in the boat.

That only left . . . What? Anything to hold water, she thought, trying to handle it logically. As she stared down into the bilge, where the icy currents were now above her ankles, her eyes widened. Shoes! Of course! If they held feet, they could also hold water.

She had them off in an instant—one in each hand—and, kneeling precariously in the center of the craft, started sloshing water over the side.

With any luck, and if her makeshift plug held in the hole, she might just keep afloat until a vessel came down the shipping lanes of the strait. The slim chance of that happening, and how she'd ever manage to get their attention, didn't bear thinking about.

She bailed again, wishing for the first time in her life that she wore shoes three sizes larger. At least the action gave her something to do rather than just cling to the seat and dwell on how terrible the chances for a rescue really were and wonder if there would be anything left to cling to when the dinghy eventually swamped. The only way she could keep from dissolving into hysteria was to concentrate on her bailing routine and try to make sure that the water didn't get any deeper.

She succeeded so well that when a hail came over the water and a searchlight started sweeping the swells just ahead of her, she thought that she was having hallucinations.

Then the brilliant light flashed over her, went just beyond, and homed back to illuminate her disbelieving, ghostlike face. From afar, there was the sound of powerful engines shutting down to a barely perceptible rumble, and while she was wondering if Lightner had decided to swing back and finish the job, a masculine voice shouted across the dark expanse of water.

"Jessica! Hang on! We're coming alongside with a rope ladder to pick you up. Don't do anything stupid, for God's sake!"

Jessica collapsed into the bottom of the dinghy and closed her eyes in a moment of thanksgiving. Later on, she'd give Cal Sloane hell for assuming she didn't have a brain in her head, but right then, it was as if the heavens had opened and showered her with golden trumpets.

When she opened her eyes again, they widened with alarm. Beyond the two searchlights that were keeping her spotlighted, she could glimpse the outlines of a good-size ship. Definitely not a pleasure craft, she thought, and clung even tighter as the swells increased when it edged closer. She watched her shoes disappear as a big wave sloshed over the bow, and thought dispassionately that she might be around to watch the swamping, after all.

"Jessica!" Cal's voice was much closer and even more ragged then. "We're throwing you a line—look alive!"

Almost on the last word, a nylon line snaked onto her shoulders and she let go of the seat with one hand to clutch it.

"Good girl! Hang on."

Things happened so fast then that she acted instinctively. The line became taut and the dinghy was pulled unceremoniously against a gray metal hull. At the same time, two sailors on rope netting thrown over the side reached down and dragged her up beside them.

Jessica felt them pushing her upward toward the rail and managed to say breathlessly, "It's all right—I can do it."

"Just take it easy, lady. You're almost there."

And Jessica, who would have climbed Mt. Everest by then to escape from that dinghy, pulled herself up and over the rail to flop like a landed fish on the metal deck.

After that, there were a dozen hands to help her to her feet again. As soon as she became vertical, she heard someone close by say in a hushed monotone, "My God! That was a close one." Her glance followed the rest of the crew's as they watched the dinghy move sluggishly away from the ship. One moment it followed the crest of a swell, and then, as they watched, it slid slowly beneath the surface of the dark, oily-looking water.

As it went, Jessica realized that she very well might have gone down with it and that her worst fears had been realized—there wasn't anything left of the fragile craft.

For the first time, she allowed reality to invade her consciousness, and the enormity was too much for her to handle. With only an apologetic whimper, she collapsed into the arms of her nearest rescuer.

Afterward she was to proclaim that it wasn't an honest-to-goodness fainting spell. She knew very well what was going on—it was just that it all seemed as if she was observing it from a seat in the bleachers, far away from the action.

That was why she didn't object when she was carried belowdecks and put on the bunk in a cabin that was small but immaculate. She did surface long enough to protest that she'd get the blankets wet since her clothes were clinging to her. At least what clothes she had left; she'd sacrificed her skirt and shoes long before. Her eyes widened when she felt her clammy slip being peeled off, and when she discovered that it was Cal doing the peeling, she opened her mouth to protest.

"Don't start arguing," he advised, and having dragged the slip off, reached for the clasp of her bra. When she indignantly tried to push his hands away, he merely remarked, "I've seen the female form before, and a United States Coast Guard cutter sure as hell isn't the place I'd pick to seduce you. God knows what the taxpayers and congressional committees would say if they caught wind of that." He did relent afterward to reach for two Turkish towels hanging on a chrome bar near the bunk. He draped one over her shoulders, saying, "This will help preserve your modesty if you feel it's important." Then he shed his impersonal attitude for a moment after surveying her still figure. "I must say that you look a hell of a lot better in a towel than most people."

"Thanks a lot," she mumbled, knowing that he was simply talking to keep her mind off what had happened. "You don't have to keep trying to be so polite."

A reluctant grin came over his face. "You mean it shows?"

"Something like that."

He was dabbing at the damp ends of her hair almost absently with the second towel. "Probably because I'd like to whale the living daylights out of you for getting into such a predicament. Are you going to take off the rest of your clothes or do I have to do it?"

Even in her traumatic state, Jessica decided things had gone far enough. She pushed up on the bunk, clutching the bath towel to her breast, and glared at him. "As you very well know, all that's left is one pair of nylon briefs, and they're practically dry already. You've done more than enough, thanks."

Her annoyed response brought a reluctant grin. "You must be feeling better," he said. "Lean forward and I'll get your circulation going again."

He'd started toweling her back before Jessica could think of a good reason to object, and the brisk rotary motion brought a surge of warmth to her skin. "That feels good," she whispered, suddenly shy at finding herself wedged against him. When a knock came on the cabin door, she gave a startled leap that almost had her in his lap.

"I'm sorry," she said, pushing back on the mattress and trying to keep a firm grip on her towel. "I'm still a little shaky."

"Just relax," Cal said, getting to his feet and tossing his towel on the blanket. "This must be room service."

She stared wide-eyed when he pulled open the cabin door and was handed a tray with two steaming mugs of coffee on it. "Captain's compliments, sir," she heard.

"Thanks very much. This should do the trick," Cal replied pleasantly, and closed the door again, balancing the tray carefully as he did it.

Jessica forgot the fact that she was freezing and practically naked on a strange bunk to ask, "What's going on? What captain was he talking about?"

"The Coast Guard captain who commands this cutter," Cal replied, waiting for her to lean back against the pillows before handing her the mug of coffee. "You're lying on his bunk."

Jessica found that it wasn't easy to try to hold the towel in place and handle a steaming mug of coffee as well.

Cal grinned as he saw her predicament. "Looks as if one or the other will have to go."

"No way. Here—hang on to the coffee for a minute," she instructed, and managed to wrap the towel, sarong fashion, so that it was more secure. "There."

"Spoilsport." Cal's look was unrepentant but he didn't waste any time handing her back the coffee mug. "Better drink this. Your teeth are still chattering."

Jessica obediently took a swallow and then rested the mug against her cheek, savoring the warmth it brought. "It feels better outside than in," she confessed as he frowned. "My stomach hasn't settled down yet. It's a good thing that I didn't drink the gin." On seeing his frown deepen, she explained. "That was the only thing Bruce let me keep in the dinghy."

Cal sank onto the mattress beside her, his own coffee forgotten. "At least you had the motor." He looked disbelieving as she shook her head.

"A motor with no gas," she told him, unaware that her knuckles were white on the coffee mug as she recalled that interlude of horror. "And a dinghy that he'd stripped for his smuggling operations."

"What do you mean?"

"He'd removed the foam flotation from under the seat earlier to carry some special cargo, he said. Actually he seemed quite proud of his accomplishment."

Cal swore softly. "So that's why it went down so fast when that last wave caught it. My God! You could have been—"

"Killed," Jessica finished the sentence, and pushed her coffee mug blindly at him as she rested her face in her hands. "That did occur to me."

Cal put both mugs on a nearby locker as if he couldn't face the thought of anything to drink, either. Then he sat beside her again to ask, "Why in the devil did you go with him in the first place?" When Jessica raised her head and broke into wild laughter, he caught her shoulders to give her a hard shake. "Stop that! If you keep it up, there'll be a corpsman down here to put you under for a while. I talked them out of it earlier, but hysterics will bring him on the run."

"Oh, God, no!" Jessica sobered immediately and drew an uneven breath. "I'll be all right—I promise."

"I know you will be," Cal told her in comforting terms. "It won't be long now until we dock at Friday Harbor and you can put all this behind you."

"You mean that we're not chasing after Bruce?" Jessica asked in alarm as she sat up straight again.

"They are—we're not," Cal told her. Then, taking

pity on her confusion, he said, "Bruce has had two Coast Guard cutters on his stern since he left the Institute. This one and a sister ship. We dropped back to investigate the dinghy launching, and they've gone on to make the arrest when he meets his 'business' associates."

"Maybe he'll turn off his running lights again."

"They're tracking him on radar," Cal explained "It doesn't matter if he turns off all his lights, there's still that reflector up on his mast. Don't worry, he won't get away this time. There's even aircraft surveillance on this mission. The only thing the authorities didn't count on was having to rescue a redhead in the middle of the action." At her crestfallen expression, he bestowed a crooked grin. "That's okay. Having you aboard probably rattled Bruce so much that he forgot to take all the precautions he normally would. Besides, you weren't the only one to find trouble. I'm not particularly proud after letting them get the drop on me at the beach that night."

"What were you doing there in the first place?"

He shrugged. "We suspected they were using your family's place for their deliveries. They couldn't have chosen a better one—it was an isolated area complete with dock so that it could be approached from two ways."

"But Henry was living in the house."

"Henry was in it up to his ears," Cal said, not bothering to hide his disgust. "He's finally owned up to it, and since he's willing to tell all, he's hoping to get off with just having his knuckles rapped, or a suspended sentence."

It was almost too much for Jessica to comprehend. "But he isn't the type at all. Why? For heaven's sake—why?"

"Money. His research funds were about to be cut and he had some farfetched idea of financing the project himself. Even then, he probably wouldn't have gone through with it if it hadn't been for Valerie." As Jessica's eyes widened, Cal said, "Oh, yes. Henry wasn't averse to having a good-looking woman fuss over him. And you must admit that Valerie plays the part very well."

"It seemed to me that she was convincing some others too."

Cal grinned momentarily at her wry comment. "All in the line of duty, I assure you. She laid it on too thick and asked too many questions, but we felt she was a valuable contact."

"You mean she was in cahoots with Bruce all along? Even when she was leading Henry down the path?"

"You've got it," Cal said, nodding. "Bruce has been under suspicion for months, but we couldn't get any proof. It was only after Henry got caught in that fire and had time to think things over in the hospital that the case began to break."

"But why did he get caught in the fire? I understand he wasn't even in the house when it started."

"Was started," Cal corrected. "Henry had developed pangs of conscience, and Bruce decided to show him what could happen if he didn't follow orders. Henry dived back into the flames to try to save some of his research data. You don't need two of those." The last comment came when Cal reached over to appropriate one of her pillows. He moved to the foot of the bunk and shoved the pillow behind his head as he leaned against the bulkhead facing her. "That's better. The Coast Guard apparently doesn't believe in too much comfort. Now, where was I?"

"Telling about Valerie and Bruce. She was the one

who got me out to the Institute in the first place tonight, with a cock-and-bull story," Jessica said disgustedly. "I should have known she was in the mess up to her neck."

"Nobody expected you to be clairvoyant," Cal said.

"Yes, but she didn't look or act like an ordinary secretary. Even her perfume was expensive, and that's what really should have tipped me off. It was all over the place tonight, and I smelled it up in Henry's condo earlier. That proved she was involved in the break-in." She shook her head in disgust. "I just wasn't thinking."

"Join the party," Cal said. "I thought you couldn't be in any danger tonight after I left you, and then you slipped through our net by that other path to the parking lot."

"I know." Jessica tucked the towel around her more securely as it started to slip. "You can credit Valerie with that maneuver. I hope that she doesn't get a sympathetic jury when she comes to trial. Anybody dealing in dope doesn't deserve one."

Cal fixed Jessica with a quizzical look. "I agree with you on that, but this isn't a drug bust."

"But I thought you said—" She broke off as he shook his head.

"No, *you* said it, and it was easier to let it ride at the time. Shipments of dope would have aroused suspicion at the Institute. The bulk alone would have made the transfers too dangerous. Besides, Henry wouldn't have gone along with that. In his strange logic, it seemed more acceptable to be involved with illegal computer chips."

"Computer chips!" Jessica exploded. "Oh, for Lord's sake. I thought it was something really important."

"It's important, all right. I'm talking about classified computer chips—the kind that the Department of Defense doesn't allow to be exported to certain countries."

Her eyes widened. "You mean high-tech Silicon Valley stuff?"

"Now you've got it."

"So there's lots of money involved," she said, thinking aloud. "I'll bet the chips were in that briefcase Bruce had under his arm." Her gaze came up to meet Cal's "What do you suppose they'd be worth?"

"To the right party—say, a couple of million or so. To our national defense"—he shook his head—"you can't put a price on it."

She thought about it for an instant and then said in a quiet voice, "Dear God, I hope they catch him."

"They will," Cal reassured her. "You look as if you're feeling better."

"I am, thanks. No, don't get up," she instructed when he shifted and looked as if he were going to. "There are a couple of other questions."

"Okay, but make them fast. You're supposed to be resting."

She waved that aside. "You've never explained why you were involved in this in the first place. Are you some sort of brass with the Pentagon or the CIA?"

He shook his head. "You're not even close. I said that you'd never make it reading tea leaves." As her eyes narrowed, he grinned and relented. "I'm in computers. Sort of a consultant, so that lets me roam around and help out the authorities from time to time. My job also provided an excuse for taking an extended vacation up here without arousing suspicion. Since I'd known Henry in college, he introduced me around and I just had to buy some real estate to make Bruce's acquaintance."

Jessica frowned as she thought about that. "You didn't mention that you owned any real estate on the island."

"Actually," he pointed out, "you didn't ask." And then, when the silence lengthened between them, he grinned again and admitted, "I'm your landlord at the moment."

"The condo? Where I'm staying?" Her voice went up in amazement. "That belongs to you?"

"Signed, sealed, and delivered." Then, seeing her disturbed expression, he said, "What's the matter? Don't you like the place?"

"It's gorgeous," she admitted. "But why did you put me in it?"

A whimsical look passed over his face. "At first, I told myself that I wanted to keep an eye on you and that was the best way to do it."

"You mean I was under suspicion too?"

He shrugged. "Look at it my way. You turned up at the crucial moment in the scenario. Henry was occupying your house, after all."

"But it was burned down."

"That hasn't stopped people before, and you admitted that it was fully covered by insurance."

"But it was my grandmother's house—"

"I know that now," he said. "And it only took that first day for you to change my mind. After that, I wanted to make sure you were safe, and I didn't take time to investigate why."

"But now you have?" Jessica was so intent on his answer that suddenly all the other things faded away: the crowded little cubicle of a room, the hard bunk, even the plain white institutional towel that she was clutching so tightly.

"Oh, yes. I'd fallen in love with you." Cal's voice

wasn't quite steady as he said, "When I saw you looking like a drowned rat in that damned dinghy . . ." He broke off and shook his head, unable to go on.

Robert Browning might not have approved of the style, but even he couldn't have faulted the sincerity of that declaration. To Jessica, Cal's words were pure gold and made her forget everything except the man with the drawn, tired face who was staring at her.

Her next comment merely served to draw out the cherished moment. "You didn't look as if you were in love. You didn't sound like it either. I thought you couldn't wait to get out of my sight."

"Then you'd better not plan on a career of reading crystal balls either."

"But you hardly made a move toward me—except in the boat, and that was just to provide a red herring for Bruce." As he started to grin, she eyed him calculatingly. "It was deliberate, wasn't it? You're an overbearing, no-good . . ." She broke off as the towel started to slip when she sat forward.

He waited, amused, and made no effort to help as she pulled it back into place. Finally he said, "There had to be some perks with the job. You'll remember that I was a perfect gentleman when I spent the night with you."

"Only because you were under the weather and suffering."

"But not exclusively from that knock on the head. You were too damned close at hand. Even those pills couldn't help with that problem. I had to keep telling myself that I was thinking in terms of a lifetime instead of a weekend."

"You mean marriage?" she asked softly, getting the words out with difficulty.

"Of course I mean marriage," Cal said, his eyebrows drawing together. "I thought that was agreed."

"You didn't ask," she pointed out.

"If you want, I'll go down on my knees, although I'm not sure if there's enough room in here," he said, looking around the tiny cabin.

"It isn't necessary," she said, scarcely able to believe what she was hearing. "I accept with pleasure. Actually, I've been going round the bend trying to figure out how to stay close to you. It all started about the time you gave me that first ticking-off on the ferry."

Her sudden smile as she admitted it was so lovely that Cal drew an unsteady breath. "Then we'd better get back to the condo, phone your brother, and start planning our wedding. Where do you want to go for a honeymoon?"

"I'd like to stay right on the island where it all began," she said dreamily.

"You're sure?" Cal's expression turned solemn. "You'll have to testify against Lightner and the rest later on. As well as file corroborative statements. That's hardly a romantic background."

"It doesn't matter—there'll be lots more good memories than bad ones."

"And there's still that uninvited guest roaming around," Cal reminded her. "I think I caught a glimpse of him by the washing machine. He was small and green and muttered something like 'Ribbet' when I tried to get a hand on him."

"We'll have to make sure and invite him to the wedding. I think that settles almost everything." Jessica fixed Cal with a stern look. "Did it occur to you that you're a great distance away for a prospective bridegroom?"

"It hasn't been out of my mind since I caught my first glimpse of you on that damned ferry." He gestured around them. "Now we end up on a U.S. Coast Guard cutter, where you're supposed to be taking it easy. I'm trying very hard to keep it in mind."

Jessica appeared to consider their plight and then said solemnly, "Perhaps you could kiss me in a very subdued way."

"Subdued, hell!" Cal moved up beside her and pulled her into his arms so fast that his pillow fell on the floor. "Darling, darling Jess—I didn't think this day would ever come."

"That makes two of us," she confessed. "I can hardly believe it's really happening—I've dreamed about it for so long." And then, as his lips fiercely parted hers, and her towel was pushed away, she forgot about thinking at all.

It was much later when he drew back just far enough to ask in deep, unsteady tones, "Dearest, I wasn't too rough on you, was I? After all, you're supposed to be resting."

Jessica observed him provocatively through half-closed lids. "I like 'resting' with you, my love, and I'm feeling much better." Then she stretched slowly, like a satisfied kitten, and traced the outline of his mouth with a soft finger. "So let's just start at the top and do it all over again."

About the Author

Glenna Finley is a native of Washington State. She earned her degree from Stanford University in Russian Studies and in Speech and Dramatic Arts, with emphasis on radio.

After a stint in radio and publicity work in Seattle, she went to New York City to work for NBC as a producer in its international division. In addition, she worked with the "March of Time" and *Life* magazine.

As a producer, she had her own show about activities in Manhattan, a show that was broadcast to England. The programs were similar to those of the "Voice of America."

Though her life in New York was exciting, she eventually returned to the Northwest where she married. She loves to travel, and draws heavily on her travels and experiences for the novels that have been published. Her books for New American Library have sold several million copies.